CAUGHT SNEAKING!

Ki had brought both candles and matches, and now he lit one. "I'd better keep it down low. There are no window shades or curtains on that big front window," he said.

Jessie's hand was sliding open the drawer as she turned to glance at the window. "Yes, that—"

The explosion blew out the front of the drawer and knocked her down. Jessie felt a sharp pain in her left hand. She tasted gunpowder and smoke as she struck the floor. "Ki," she whispered weakly as she began to lose consciousness. "We have to get out of here!"

Ki could see the twin smoking barrels protruding from where the front of the desk drawer had been. "Jessie!"

WESLEY ELLIS

LONE STAR

AND THE TEXAS RANGERS

J

JOVE BOOKS, NEW YORK

LONE STAR AND THE TEXAS RANGERS

A Jove book/published by arrangement with
the author

PRINTING HISTORY
Jove edition/December 1988

ISBN: 0-515-09848-5

Jove books are published by The Berkley Publishing Group,
200 Madison Avenue, New York, New York 10016.
The name "JOVE" and the "J" logo
are trademarks belonging to Jove Publications, Inc.

PRINTED IN THE UNITED STATES OF AMERICA

10 9 8 7 6 5 4 3 2 1

Chapter 1

Jessica Starbuck saw the cow and her calf break from the herd and head for the thickets. She touched her spurs to her palomino, Sun, and the big horse darted after the cow. Jessie would have to overtake and rope the wild longhorns before they reached the thickets or they would be free until next spring's big Circle Star roundup. Jessie's hemp rope whirled overhead so fast it whistled, and then her arm flicked forward and the noose shot out like a living fist. It settled neatly over the cow's wide, sweeping horns. Jessie reined Sun hard left. The rope went taut and cut the longhorn's back legs out from under its body at the same time it hit the end of the line. The running cow somersaulted up into the air and then crashed to the earth with such shocking impact that it was temporarily stunned.

Jessie moved her horse forward a little and gave the cow slack. Its fine brindle calf bawled with anxious confusion as it stared wide-eyed at its mother.

"Mama is going to be all right, little fella," Jessie said, a smile creasing her generous lips. Jessie tipped back her Stetson to reveal her thick, copper-colored hair. Her man's shirt was unbuttoned at the throat and tapered to a nice swell over her breasts. Jessie sleeved perspiration off her forehead. She knew her face was grimy from the dust and sweat of the roundup and she wished there was more of an afternoon breeze to cool things down a little. "Come on, Mama," she said encouragingly, "you know us females

1

can't be caught lying flat on our backs in this rough country. It just isn't safe, and it sure as the devil isn't proper."

The cow struggled weakly to its feet. It was still a little dazed and wobbly, but now that Jessie had taught it a hard lesson, the cow would never try to quit the herd again. Its calf trailed along behind, one more addition to the great herd that Jessie owned and raised on her huge Texas ranch, the Circle Star.

"Miss Starbuck!"

Jessie turned in her saddle to see her bronc-buster, Billy Trevors, come galloping up to her. He was riding a young horse, which was taking a hard buck about every third stride. Billy was riding the horse as if it were child's play. He had a letter in his hand and Jessie could not imagine why he would bother her with correspondence out on the roundup. She had a secretary for that sort of thing, and . . .

"It's marked personal and urgent, Miss Starbuck," the cowboy explained as if reading her thoughts. The green-broke horse under him was covered with foam, still dancing and looking as if it were ready to explode.

"You sure didn't need to go to all the trouble of bringing it clear out here," Jessie said.

Billy quieted the bronc, but not viciously. "Well, Miss Starbuck, I asked the cooks and none of them had any idea what to do so I took it to your samurai."

"And he said?"

"Ki said you should see it immediately. So here I am." He shoved the letter at Jessie. "It's from Cap'n Ray in Austin."

"Take the rope," Jessie said, flipping the end of it to the cowboy in exchange for the letter. Billy grabbed the rope and tied it hard and fast around his saddlehorn. "This here bronc is going to be a regular cow pony before sunset," he said, trying to keep the bronc from exploding into the sky instead of leading the cow back to the herd.

2

Jessie stared at the letter. She had a bad premonition about letters marked this way. "You did the right thing. I guess you know that the captain is like part of my family."

Billy nodded. He started to lead the cow the rest of the way back to the herd where the calf would be branded with the famous Circle Star. "I just hope the cap'n is all right, ma'am. He's pretty special to all of us."

It was right about then that the bronc erupted up toward the sky. Billy quirted it hard and dug in his spurs. The bronc grunted in pain but stubbornly kept bucking. The rope got tangled up behind its rear legs and that made the bronc fight even harder. The cow began to bawl. All the fight was out of it because of the way Jessie had busted it to the ground. But with the rope around its neck now tied to Billy's saddlehorn, the cow was being jerked every which way but loose. Its tongue was hanging out and its eyes were bugged. It was clear it was being choked half to death. Two cowboys came racing in and one of them yelled, "Quit showboatin', dammit, Billy! Untie the rope and let us handle things before you break its fool neck!"

Billy wasn't showboating at all. He had the look of a man who needed about six hands and had only two. But somehow he did manage to untie his rope and set the cow free before its neck was jerked from its body. The grateful cow streaked for the safety of the big roundup herd and its calf went right along after it. Billy rode the bronc to a standstill, big clouds of dust pumping up from the dry earth. Billy was putting on one hell of a fine ride but nobody paid the bronc-buster the slightest bit of attention. This was roundup time and with the roping, doctoring of sick cattle, riding, castrating, and branding, not one of the thirty Circle Star cowboys had time to enjoy watching an expert bronc-buster display his talents. And Jessie was too busy opening the letter.

3

Billy, glancing over and realizing he and the bronc were putting on a show that wasn't even being watched much less appreciated, finished the bronc off with some hard spurring. The horse lit out at a run toward the ranch headquarters. Its dust hung like a hazy brown curtain in the hot Texas air.

Jessie had removed her gloves and now she unfolded the letter and began to read what amounted to little more than a terse note. It said: "Dear Jessie: I figure this is your roundup time and I hate like blazes to bother you but I need help bad. Can't explane now just in case this litter should fall into the wrong hands before it gits to yors. Sorry for being a pest."

It was signed Captain Ben F. Ray, of the Texas Rangers, Texas Ranger Headquarters, Austin, Texas.

Jessie read the letter twice. When she folded it up and put it into the front pocket of her shirt, her green eyes were troubled. Captain Ben, as she called him, had been a dear friend of her father's for nearly twenty years. As a young man, Captain Ben had proven himself one of the most gallant Texas Rangers ever to pin a badge on his vest. He had joined that elite fighting force just after the fall of the Alamo. Sharing the outrage of all Texans, he had been a part of Sam Houston's rag-tag little army which had outfoxed and out-fought the Mexicans and defeated General Santa Anna at the Battle of San Jacinto. Ben Ray had served as a Texas Ranger with great distinction. He had fought Kiowa, Comanche, and Mexican raiders for years. In 1846, he'd been one of the chosen Texas Rangers who had served as scouts and as an elite cavalry force during the Mexican War. He'd fought side by side with the famed Captain Samuel Walker as Zack Taylor and his soldiers had gone into Mexico City and forced Santa Anna to cede California, Arizona, New Mexico, and most of Colorado to the

United States in return for fifteen million dollars and a peaceful withdrawal of the victorious American forces.

Yes, Captain Ben Ray along with a special few other old Texas Rangers like Semus Jones were legends in their own time. With this fresh in Jessie's mind, it made the case for urgency even more obvious. When a legend was in trouble —and a Texas Ranger to boot—that meant something was very, very wrong.

Jessie galloped Sun over to her foreman, Ed Wright. The tall, weather-beaten cattleman had been with Jessie for years and could be counted on to finish off the roundup without a hitch. He had obviously been watching her read the letter, and he was old and wise enough to know that something was very much amiss. "Big trouble," he said. It was not a question.

"Yes," Jessie replied. "Captain Ben needs my help. I'll be taking Ki with me and leaving for Austin at once."

"Anything I can do for you?"

"No," Jessie said. "When the roundup is over, trail the two thousand head we discussed over to San Antonio and sell them to the cattle buyers."

"No long drive up to Abilene or Dodge City this year?"

"Not this year," Jessie told him. "That's why we're selling so few. Next year we'll all trail north and have some fun."

"What about Ki?" Ed asked with the slightest trace of a grin. "You know how your samurai hates playing cowboy for months at a time."

"I know," Jessie replied. "Maybe I'll have him study oriental cooking and help out old Shorty Blevins in the chuck wagon."

Ed Wright blinked and was not quite able to keep his face from revealing how poor an idea he thought that was. Cowboys would not eat oriental cooking; but then, he suspected Jessie knew that and was putting him on. Playing it

5

straight, Ed nodded his head and said, "Sounds like a hell of an idea, Miss Starbuck. Well, I better get back to work. Give the cap'n my best. I sure hope whatever is wrong can be taken care of pronto."

"So do I," Jessie said, turning Sun back toward ranch headquarters and following the still faint dust trail of Billy Trevors. "So do I."

Circle Star was a sprawling cattle empire in southwestern Texas that had been built by Alex Starbuck and had given him great joy during the last years of his illustrious and amazing life. Like everything else related to her father, the headquarters was a monument to the Starbuck legend. Huge and sprawling, it was all Texas, big, wide and handsome. Not gaudy or with false show, however. Alex had loved to make and spend money but he had never given a damn about impressing anyone. He had built his empire from a small import-export shop in San Francisco. As his talent as a businessman and entrepreneur became apparent on the ledger sheets of his surprisingly successful shop, Alex expanded by purchasing a battered sailing ship to carry goods from the Orient to the United States. His one ship soon became two, then three, then a fleet of merchant trading vessels that expanded his horizons to all points of the globe.

Not only had Alex Starbuck been a daring business-man, constantly challenging himself to new and more profitable ventures, he had also been a visionary. He had acquired a small shipyard and been one of the very first men who had dared to build new ships with steel rather than wooden hulls. Once other fleet owners had seen how fast and durable the revolutionary Starbuck fleet was, they had begun to order ships from their competitor, Alex Starbuck. Business had become so brisk that Alex had bought his own steel mill as well as mines to supply the mill with ores. A few years later when the railroads had become

6

enormously profitable and new lines were reaching out across America like the tentacles of an octopus, Alex had become a major supplier of rail and plate for locomotive boilers. Not content merely to supply the steel for the locomotive age, Alex had invested heavily in railroad stock just as the value of railroads bloomed. He had made millions of dollars and had reinvested it in banking and brokerage.

By the time he was fifty, Alex Starbuck had become recognized as one of the richest and most powerful men in the world. He had purchased companies on every continent of the world, and his combined payrolls were, though secret, estimated to be far greater than that of entire countries. Through it all, Alex had remained almost boyish in his delight and desire to improve the lot of all mankind. He had never bought a company for which he did not raise wages and morale. He personally inspected the living quarters of employees in the less developed countries and insisted that they receive education for their children, good diet, and medical care. Alex had been loved, and was called a humanitarian, though he eschewed praise and had always considered himself first and foremost a businessman. He had sent his daughter to Eastern finishing schools, but in the end, before he had been murdered by a vicious cartel of European industrialists intent on demolishing his far-flung empire, Alex had loved Circle Star and cattle ranching most of all.

"Good afternoon, Miss Starbuck," a ranch hand not yet out of his teens said, as Jessie dismounted in front of the sprawling ranch house. "How's the roundup goin' today?"

Jessie handed him her reins. "Just fine, Ted. Maybe next year, if you improve on your roping a little more, you can be a part of it."

Ted beamed. "You know I practice every chance I get. I'll be ready next year."

7

Jessie nodded. Ted wanted to be a cowboy more than anything else in the world. His father had been a top hand but had been gored to death by a wild longhorn in the brush. His mother had died of a broken heart and Ted would have a home and a paycheck for life as long as he was willing to work and better himself. Jessie, like her father, appreciated loyalty even more than talent. You could buy talent just like you could buy whiskey, eggs, or a good horse. Talent was always available to the highest bidder. But loyalty, that was a rarer quality that could never be bought—only earned.

Jessie started for the house. "I know you're practicing a lot," she called back over her shoulder to Ted, who would rub down Sun and put him in a clean stall. "Every dog, cat, and chicken on the place runs when it sees a rope in your hands."

Ted laughed. A high, happy laugh that made Jessie grin. She liked that boy. She had liked his father and his mother, too.

"Where's Ki?" she asked a houseworker as she entered the door.

The young Mexican girl pointed to the study, curtseyed and hurried away, her skirts making soft, brushing sounds accompanied by the pat-pat of her leather sandals on the Spanish floor tiles.

Juanita was also an orphan, the daughter of a Mexican *vaquero* who had been killed several years ago in a horse fall. Juanita was pretty and spoke good English, but she was very shy. Someday soon, Jessie hoped, she would gain more self-assurance. Juanita was secretly in love with young Ted. And unless Jessie read the wrong messages, he was smitten with her as well.

"Too young by three years at least," Jessie said to herself as she hurried into the study.

"Too young for what?" Ki asked, turning to face her.

8

Jessie waved her hand with distraction. Ki was her best friend, protector, and advisor, just as he had been to Alex Starbuck. Ki was ageless and a wonder. He was a samurai and the most remarkable man Jessie had ever known.

"Too young to marry for at least three years," Jessie said.

"You mean young Ted and Señorita Mendoza?"

"Yes," Jessie said. "May I read you the letter?"

Ki nodded.

Jessie reread it aloud very quickly. When she finished, she looked up at the samurai, who was watching her closely. Ki was Eurasian, son of an American sailor and a Japanese woman of nobility. He had inherited his father's height and lean gracefulness, but his features and the color of his skin made him appear Oriental. And because he had been raised in Japan, his dress reflected much of that culture. Being a samurai, he wore a loose black pajamalike costume, rope sandals, and a headband to keep his long black hair in place. His cheekbones were high and his eyes were large and olive-shaped. He was a beautiful man, slender but very strong, and incredibly graceful and quick. Had he not been sworn to protect Jessie at the expense of his own life, he might have been her lover.

Jessie put down the letter. "I want to leave within the hour."

"I expected you would. I am ready."

"How did you expect anything?"

The samurai shrugged. "When Billy showed the letter to me, I told him to take it to you at once. If there was not big trouble in Austin, why else would a Texas Ranger send for help?"

There were times when Ki was so logical that it wore on Jessie's nerves. His mind was like a filing system. He seemed to miss nothing, hear everything. See everything. Like a samurai.

"Yes," she said, heading for her bedroom to pack a small valise.

Ki said, "I can have your carriage ready."

Jessie stopped and turned. "No," she decided. "I think we can get to Austin faster on horseback. And that being the case, I had better tell Ted to go out to the tackroom and get my saddlebags."

"Not required, Jessie." The samurai reached behind him and took Jessie's saddlebags from a chair. "I anticipated that you'd want to ride there and took the liberty of getting these cleaned and oiled. You'll also find I've packed your six-gun and some extra rounds of ammunition inside as well."

Jessie shook her head. "Sometimes you make me feel like a little girl."

"I try to keep you humble. And since you are rich, beautiful, and wise, that is not always easy," the samurai told her.

Jessie took the saddlebags and headed for her bedroom. She had never met such a man as Ki, and just once in a great while, she thought that it was just as well. His will and intelligence were at least equal to her own. Jessie was not sure that two equals made a perfect match. Perhaps they could discuss this on the long ride to Austin.

It was a desolate ride across hard, monotonous country. There might be nothing better to do than to match wits with her samurai. That way, they would both be sharp and ready for whatever Captain Ben Ray had waiting for them at the headquarters of the Texas Rangers.

Chapter 2

As they galloped east, the country greened up some and they crossed the San Antonio and then the Guadalupe looking at grass still holding moisture despite it being midsummer. There were times that Jessie wondered why her father had established his cattle empire down in the southwest of Texas rather than in the central or eastern part of the state where the country was prettier and there was more water. But Alex had never done anything without a good purpose in mind and Jessie had grown to love the dry, hard land on which it might take twenty or thirty acres to feed a cow and her calf. Besides, down where her ranch covered more land than could be ridden in a week, you had a sense of vastness that was unparallelled anywhere in the world.

Since Alex Starbuck's murder by the cartel, Jessie had been forced to leave Texas and Circle Star far more often than she liked. Had she wished, she could have sold her father's vast industrial empire, piece by piece, and devoted her entire energies to Circle Star. But she found that, even though leaving cattle country was hard sometimes, she loved to travel and meet other peoples and learn about other cultures. It always renewed her spirit to travel and see that the hope of the world depended on nations working together to trade and gain mutual economic benefits. In America, the country was entering a real industrial age and Jessie knew that the success of Circle Star would always be dependent upon her willingness to experiment and to move forward. To that end, she had been a strong and persistent advocate of introducing new purebred English beef breeds into the West. And when she had crossbred Hereford and Angus with her longhorns, she had produced a superior meat animal. Not that she had yet been able to convince the American consumer on a large scale of the superiority of her cattle; but she wasn't the only one moving in that direction. Up north, the famous old trailblazer, Charles Goodnight, had also introduced Angus into his herds and had even crossed them with buffalo, which resulted in a strange-looking creature he called the "cattloe."

Change. You either went with it, or it steamrolled you and left you behind.

"Look up ahead," Ki said. "There's a woman in trouble down by that little stream."

Jessie saw her at once. She was tall and thin and running from a big man. Behind them was a wagon parked beside a thick stand of cottonwood trees. The woman's long hair was flying and she was trying to escape, but the big man, in his early thirties, caught her by the hair and wrestled her to the earth. As he struggled to pull the woman's dress up over her head, it was very clear that his intentions were dishonorable.

"Let's go!" Jessie said.

They were just a mile off and yet it seemed to take the longest time before they reached the pair. Despite the fact that the man was large and strong-looking, he had not succeeded in getting the dress up above her knees.

"Get off of her!" Jessie yelled.

The man would not get off the thin, very homely woman.

Ki leaped off his horse and ran forward. He did not even break stride as he sent a perfectly timed sweep-kick that caught the man under the chin and lifted him off the woman. The man rolled and, head down, arms out-stretched, he recovered enough to lunge at Ki.

The samurai appeared to move almost indolently. He took his time until the very last instant, when he ducked the outreached arms that wanted to crush and break him. And as the man stumbled past, Ki sent a flat-foot kick to the exposed area over his kidney. The fellow staggered, his back arched, and his face went pale as he tumbled to the dirt.

Jessie was already off her horse and moving to the woman, who was in her thirties, tall, rawboned, and vaguely familiar. Jessie reached down to help and comfort her and that was when the woman pulled a derringer out of her dress pocket and said, "One move and I'll blow your goddamn brains all the way to the goddamn Rio Grande River, Miss Starbuck."

Jessie froze. Ki started to move, but then he froze too as two hidden riflemen shoved rifles out of the back of the wagon. One of them yelled. "Freeze, mister! One move and you're dead. Then Miss Starbuck is on her own."

Ki froze. He was a samurai, and his first responsibility was for Jessie's safety. If he died in a futile charge because of honor, he would actually be dishonoring himself with failure.

The woman Jessie had been about to help now stood up. Her hair was matted, her dress was faded to a dirty white, and she was in need of a bath. "Who are you?"

"Call me Matty, Miss-High-'n'-Mighty Jessica Star-buck."

"Haven't I seen you somewhere?" Jessie asked, desperately trying to place this woman and, at the same time, wondering in what way she could possibly have wronged her.

"Sure you did, but you can't remember and you never

13

will. Rich ladies like you don't want to see the likes of me. But I seen you—many times!"

The woman's voice took on a knife's sharp edge. "You was always ridin' high and fancy on that big palomino horse, or in your pretty carriage with your men gathered all around like a bunch of drone bees hovering around their goddamn queen. No, you never saw me or my family. But we all seen you and we knowed there had to be a way to bring you down to our level and spread your money out to us."

"I never hurt you or your husband or sons," Jessie said in a still voice.

The woman moved away from her a few steps. "No," she hissed, "but you sure as hell never helped any of us Beesleys, either!"

The man who had taken such a beating from Ki screamed, "Goddammit, Matty, we agreed not to give her our last names!"

Jessie had it now. "Beesleys. You people had a homestead over near San Antonio, didn't you?"

The derringer shook threateningly.

Ki said, "Jessie, don't say anything more!"

But Jessie continued. "You lost everything in the drought a few years back. But then this past winter was wet and we had good spring rains. How come—"

"Cattlemen!" the heavyset man choked. "Cattlemen drove their herds through our new cornfield and ruined the crop. There wasn't enough corn on the cobs to feed a goddamn rat! But they trampled it, by Gawd!"

"But I had nothing to do with that!" Jessie exclaimed.

"You're all the same," the woman hissed. "Doesn't matter which of you did it—all that matters is that you did it! We picked you 'cause we knowed you was headin' for Austin."

"And how did you know that?"

"We saw the letter Captain Ray sent. Envelope was thin enough to read right through the paper. It didn't take much figurin' to guess you'd bring the samurai, too. So we came to meet you, Miss Starbuck."

Jessie expelled a deep breath because now the puzzle was all in place. "And now you'll want a ransom. Is that the game you've decided to play?"

"It is."

"How much?"

Matty squared her thin shoulders. "Ten thousand dollars," she whispered, as if she had spoken a figure so high that it might not actually exist. In truth, it was a pathetically small amount of money for the risks they were taking.

"To be delivered where?"

Matty blinked and her drawn face reflected shock. "You mean you're just going to pay it? No fuss or nothin'?"

"I didn't say that," Jessie said, knowing that if she let this family—no matter how desperate and destitute they might be—get away with this ransom business, then others would be sure to try as well.

Matty's two boys came out from the back of the relic of a wagon. They were tall, winter-wolf lean, and in their mid-teens. Their clothes were rags and they had no shoes. They looked very hungry and not a little bit scared. But they also looked as if they knew how to shoot very straight. Jessie could always tell if a man could shoot well by how he carried a gun or rifle. These boys carried theirs as if they were extensions of their bodies.

Maybe Ki sensed that, too, for when the big man ordered him to lie down flat on his stomach and put his hands behind his back, Ki did as he was told. The big man drew

15

his gun. When Jessie yelled, he swung its barrel and it struck Ki right above the ear. The samurai faded.

"Damn you!" Jessie raged. "He did what you wanted. You didn't need to pistol-whip him!"

"That's not the story we hear," the man said as he knelt beside the samurai and tied his hands behind his back and then his ankles together. "We heard this Chinaman is as mean as a teased polecat and twice as quick. I guess he showed me that a few minutes ago. Like to broke my damned back!"

He looked to his two boys. "Zeb, you and Enos pick him up and throw him in the wagon. Then you sit on him until I come and tell you to do otherwise. Hear me?"

They nodded. And though Ki probably weighed only about 170 pounds fully dressed, they had to struggle to lift and carry him to the wagon, then to get him into the back of it.

"If you ever touch him again," Jessie said, now that she had their attention, "even so much as muss his hair, you can both forget any money from me. And I'll see that you are hunted down and punished no matter how long it takes."

Big Albert Beesley did not like being threatened. He stepped forward, raised his hand, and slapped Jessie hard. Her head rocked, and for an instant she actually lost consciousness, though she managed to stay on her feet.

"Don't hit her, Albert! We agreed that you're not to hit her!"

"I tell you what I'd like to do to her," the man said, studying Jessie's full breasts and how her riding pants tapered down from her shapely hips.

Matty Beesley went pale. She opened her mouth, for her husband's meaning could not have been clearer. But she clamped her thin lips together and swallowed her hurt and anger. "So what are we going to do now that we got 'em?" she managed to choke a few minutes later.

"I don't know fer sure," Albert confessed, the anger and the lust washing out of him as he toed the earth. "I guess I never figured this part out, directly. I was just worryin' about gettin' her and that Chinese fella."

"He isn't Chinese," Jessie said angrily, for she felt compelled to right an error that had always vexed the samurai. "He's half Caucasian, half—"

"Half Cau-what?"

Jessie shook her head. The Beesleys were pretty ignorant people. And while she guessed that worked to her advantage, it was trying. "Half Caucasian," she repeated. "Half white, like us."

Albert shook his head and used the toe of his ruined old work boot to tip Ki over onto his back. "He's a Chink pure and simple to me."

Jessie wanted to lunge at the stupid, brutal man and use her fingernails to rake his eyes out since she had been disarmed and could do little more. But Matty must have sensed it. She said, "You don't let my man bother you none. Let him bother me, Miss Starbuck. He's been doin' it for years and I'm used to it, sure enough."

Jessie forced her eyes away from Albert. She had decided that he was dangerous enough to kill her and Ki if his underdeveloped brain reached the conclusion that that was the safest course of action for him to follow. Matty, while she was no princess, seemed to have a little more compassion despite her rough talk and foul language. "So what are you going to do with me?"

Matty said, "Turn around while I tie your hands behind your back."

Jessie turned around when Albert pointed his gun directly in her face. She felt Matty bind her wrists together

17

but not as tightly as she might have. Not nearly as tightly as her husband had bound Ki's hands a few minutes earlier. Jessie knew that, if they were to escape, the burden was on her shoulders.

"I guess I don't know either how we're going to get the money and let you go free," Matty was saying. "I was thinking of sending Zeb to your ranch and telling them the deal, plain and simple."

"There's no one on my ranch who has the authority to write a check for ten thousand dollars," Jessie said. That was not entirely true. Ed Wright had the authority to write checks a whole lot bigger than that during her absence from the ranch. But Ed would never write a check under these circumstances. Instead, he'd grab Zeb, nail him by his ears to the barn door and beat the hell out of him until he found out where Jessie was being kept. Then Ed would gather the men and come a-running.

"Well, then, who does?"

"My banker in Austin."

"Oh no!" Albert shouted. "We aren't about to take you into the same town as your Texas Ranger friend. What do you take us for, stupid?"

"Then San Antonio," Jessie said, declining to answer the man's question. "I also have a banker in San Antonio. He'll sign the check."

The pair looked at each other. Matty spoke first. "All right, then, we start for San Antonio right now."

"But it'll be dark before we get there!" Albert protested.

"Sure it will," Matty argued. "Never mind that. We'll be waiting on the doorstep with a note for the banker when he walks up to open the place. It will work."

"It had better," Albert swore. "'Cause I'm going to be puttin' the barrel of my six-gun to the Chinaman's head every minute that you and the others are gone. And if I hear any shootin', or if the law comes runnin', I'll kill him in a second. I got nothin' more to lose but my life. And I ain't askairt of dyin' any longer."

Matty's washed-out, blue eyes softened. Her sun and wind ravaged face seemed to lose the anger and meanness that Jessie had noticed from the first moment she'd seen the woman. "I know, Pa," she told him quietly. "And I feel the same goddamn way. I just don't want the boys to get kilt, is all. We've had our chances and failed. They ain't had theirs yet."

Albert said nothing. He didn't need to. Jessie saw hatred and anger and desperation. Matty and her boys were not yet to the point of being killers, but Albert was. Jessie knew that she would have to pay the ransom or the half-crazed farmer would carry out his threat to murder Ki. *So, then, I'll pay him gladly,* she thought. *But when I do, will he suddenly take the money and kill us both anyway?*

That was the real question. A question that would have to wait until they reached San Antonio and her bank.

Jessie stepped out of the wagon. Ki was conscious but not showing it. The two boys were still guarding him closely but they were running on a thin string and nearly played out from the waiting and the mounting tension.

"It's time to finish this up," Matty said, drawing out her derringer to show to Jessie. "This will be in my pocket and I'll be right at your side all the way. Don't try to double-cross me. My husband will kill your friend if you do."

"I know," Jessie said, smoothing her dress and trying to comb her hair with her fingers. She knew that she looked terrible. Her appearance and that of the gaunt creature beside her might be enough to alert the bank president, Mr. Tilson, but Jessie knew that she could not be sure. She would have to be careful not to let that happen. Ki's life depended on her following the Beesleys' instructions to the letter and then trusting that Albert would set the samurai free.

"My boys will be watchin' too," Matty said very slowly, each word falling from her chapped lips like a pellet. "If they see anything wrong, they'll come running to Albert. If they do, your friend's blood will be on your head, not ours."

"Will your husband honor his word and not hurt Ki if I do exactly as you say and get the ten thousand dollars?" Jessie asked in a hushed voice intended for Matty's ears alone.

The woman nodded wearily. "Yep. He gave me his word on that. I made him promise. Once we got the money, we'll take you and him out on the prairie and turn you loose. All you got to worry about is Indians, and there ain't many of them out there these days."

Jessie nodded. She felt a deep sense of relief. "Then let's go and get this over with."

She headed for the bank with Matty in tow. They arrived just as Mr. Tilson was opening the doors.

"Why, Miss Starbuck!" he exclaimed. "Why you look as if . . ." He caught his words just in time. ". . . as if you've had to ride a long way in a hurry."

"I need your help . . . or rather, Mrs. Beesley does. Don't you, Mrs. Beesley?"

Matty nodded, but it was plain to see she was furious at Jessie for divulging her true last name. *The heck with her,* Jessie thought, *we aren't here on a friendly outing. This is for Ki's life.*

Tilson could not quite hide his surprise that Jessie should call such a poorly dressed and hard-used looking woman a "friend." However, he recovered well and extended his hand to Matty. "Mrs. Beesley, a pleasure to meet you. What can I do for you?"

Matty quickly glanced at Jessie for help.

Jessie waited a moment, then said, "I would like to lend Mrs. Beesley ten thousand dollars."

"Ten thousand, Miss Starbuck? That's a great deal of—"

"Right now, please," Jessie said, interrupting the banker. "We are in a hurry."

"Why, certainly," the banker said. "Step right inside, ladies. We can take care of this matter in just a few minutes."

Tilson was a man of his word. Within ten minutes, Matty had the money in her hands and they were striding back to the wagon, the boys falling in behind them.

"Did you get it?" Albert cried.

Matty looked as if she were ready to burst from joy. "You damn right I got it! Let's get out of here before something goes wrong!"

Jessie was shoved back up into the wagon and away they went. Albert did not take his eyes or the barrel of his gun off them, although he kept reaching into a canvas sack and fingering the ten thousand dollars. He also kept wetting his lips.

Matty and her boys were in the front seat and they were driving the wagon westward. Jessie looked right into Albert's eyes and said, "You mean to kill us both."

He did not reply. His silence was answer enough. Jessie's mind raced to find some way to escape. Some way to disarm Albert.

But the samurai was still tied and lying on the floor of the wagon. There had not been one second since the moment he had been bound that one of the Beesleys had not been hovering over him and watching his every breath.

21

"I think we've gone far enough to let them go now," Matty said, pulling the old wagon to a halt. "No sense in going too far out and taking a chance on the Indians getting 'em. They did their part, now it's time to do ours."

The boys hopped down and helped Matty down as well. Jessie watched the woman. It was clear she was not as strong as she appeared. In fact, she looked distinctly unwell.

Albert motioned with his gun. "Get out, Miss Starbuck."

She shook her head. "Not without Ki."

"Get out!"

Jessie grabbed the samurai and felt his muscles tense even though he still pretended to be just semi-conscious. "I'm taking him with me," she said, as Matty and the boys reached for her and Ki. "You have the money, now you just leave us be."

Matty looked at Jessie when she and Ki were out on the road. "You aren't but a few miles from town. Someone will come along before tonight and help you."

"Your husband means to murder us," Jessie said, loud enough for the whole family to hear.

Matty shook her head. "I won't let him do that. We Beesleys might be poor, and even thieves after today, but we ain't murderers. Are we, Albert?"

Albert would not meet her eyes. "You and and the boys get back in the wagon and drive on a ways. I'll be along."

But Matty shook her head. "No. You promised, and we're all holdin' you to that promise, Albert. Me and the boys are a part of this, we have a say-so, too!"

Albert backhanded her just the way he'd backhanded Jessie. And at that moment, Ki, though his hands were still tied behind his back and his ankles were bound, came off the ground like an arrow. He slammed his head into Albert's stomach and the man grunted as the air exploded from his lungs. Jessie raked at his face but Albert jumped back and drew his pistol. "Hold it right there!" he bellowed.

Ki was down and Jessie was watching Matty and her boys. "If you leave him behind, he'll murder us and you'll all hang for it. Not just him. Those boys of yours deserve a better chance at life than that."

"Poor people never git no chances!" Albert shouted. "The only chance we'll have is to kill them and then we can spend the ten thousand dollars without worrying about someone coming after us. Matty, you know I'm right."

"Don't listen to him!" Jessie argued, for it was clear now that Matty and the boys were the key to any chance at survival they might have. "He's going to get you hung, sure as the sun comes up in the morning."

Matty swallowed. She was so thin that her Adam's apple bobbed up and down in her throat. "You gave your word, Albert. And we gave ours to this woman. It ain't right."

Albert began to shake with fury. "Nothing in this world is right! People like her are rich, and they smashed our crop and starved us off our land. Land we had two babies buried on, Matty!"

"You could buy it back with the money you have. It's yours, Matty. It's yours for what the cattlemen did to your crops."

"You mean that?" the woman asked, her eyes widening a little. "You'd let us keep the money and buy back our farm?"

"I'll do that and more. I'll put out the word that no more crops are to be trampled. Ever. They'll listen to me, Matty. I give you my word."

Albert could see that he had lost the argument. He

23

shook his head violently and pulled his six-gun. "Get in the wagon!" he screamed at his wife and children.

But Matty shook her head. She stepped in front of Jessie and folded her arms across her thin chest and said, "No, Albert. I believe this woman. They'll be no killing."

Albert pistol-whipped his wife. It was a vicious blow and the front sight of his gun tore a wicked gash across Matty's cheek. The woman grabbed her face and her sons leaped forward to support her, their eyes burning with hatred directed at their father. Jessie jumped for Albert's gun and managed to get her fingers on it, but the man was too strong and he knocked her to the dirt.

"Boys, throw your mama in the wagon and drive outta here!"

The boys hesitated.

"Do as I say, damn you!" Albert screamed.

Their wills bending to that of their father, the boys did as they were told. Jessie's heart sank as the wagon rolled away, leaving her facing certain death with Albert. She tried to think of something to say, but when she looked in the farmer's eyes she knew her words would be wasted.

Suddenly, the wagon stopped and then Matty and the boys were climbing out and standing about eighty yards away in the middle of the dusty road. Matty, her face still bleeding, shouted, "Albert, you gave us your word. Now come along!"

"No!"

Matty turned and said something to her Enos and Zeb. They raised their rifles and pointed at their father.

Albert went white. He couldn't believe his eyes. Stepping toward them, he began cursing and raving. This was the first opportunity Jessie had seen since they had been captured, and she meant to make the most of it. She bent down and untied Ki's knots. The samurai came to his feet. His hand moved into his vest and found a *shuriken* blade.

"Beesley!" Ki shouted.

The man spun around with his gun. There was little question that he meant to kill them both. But he never got the chance. Ki's hand shot forward and the *shuriken* blade flashed like a silver disk and buried itself in Albert's chest. The big man released one shot; then the gun fell harmlessly from his fingers. He clawed at his chest, and he was still clawing when he toppled face down in the roadway.

Ki looked at Jessie. He sounded almost apologetic when he said, "It was better for me to do it than his own sons."

Jessie nodded. She walked past Ki and the dead farmer, and when she opened her arms, Matty collapsed in them and wept as if her heart were broken. Jessie held her close and said, "Mrs. Beesley, see that you and your boys get some new clothes and plenty to eat. Use the ten thousand dollars to buy back your homestead and improve upon it."

"God bless you!" Matty whispered.

Jessie looked past her to the two boys. "You're the men of the family now. You take care of your mother and you grow up to keep your word. Always. Do you understand that?"

They nodded. Jessie eased Matty out of her arms and turned away. She would forever wonder if Zeb and Enos would have shot their own father and saved her life. She kind of thought they would have. Matty was the strength of that family, the real foundation. Jessie sincerely hoped the boys grew up to be more like her instead of like their father.

"Let's make up some time," she said. "We still have trouble waiting for us in Austin."

Ki nodded. "It can't be any worse than this was. I pity that woman."

"I don't," Jessie said, turning to see Matty hugging her two tall sons. "I have a feeling that without Albert her life is going to be a whole lot more successful than it ever has been. She'll buy the farm free and clear, work hard, and probably remarry a far better man. Her sons stood at the fork of a big road and now I think that they are going to go in the right direction."

"You always were the optimist," Ki said.

Jessie didn't answer. She turned without even glancing at Albert Beesley again. And she began to walk, with her long arms swinging and graceful stride, back toward San Antonio. Sun was waiting, and so was Captain Ben Ray in Austin.

Chapter 3

Austin, Texas had been named the capital of the new Texas
Republic in 1839, and was now the state capital. It was
situated on a series of low hills overlooking the Colorado
River, and Jessie had always thought it was extremely pic-
turesque. Sam Houston, of course, had been miffed when
the fledgling government had been moved out of Houston,
where he'd hoped it would remain. But years later, even
the old general, senator, and statesman had finally con-
ceded that Austin was a good choice.

Ranger headquarters was spartan, just a modest building
with only a couple of private offices. Jessie saw a lot of
familiar faces when she arrived, but she was so anxious to
see Ben Ray that she barely stopped to talk with any of the
Rangers.

"So you've come to see Ben, huh?" Ranger Carl Wins-
low said.

"Yes. Is he in his office?"

"I'm afraid he's been sick this past week. He's taken to
his bed. You can visit him at home."

"I know my way there," Jessie said.

On her way out the door, several of the Rangers called
for Jessie and Ki to give Ben their best wishes. It was clear
that they thought a lot of the old lawman and wanted him
to return as soon as possible, even though age and infirmi-
ties kept him riding an office chair rather than a horse these
days.

Jessie moved swiftly to her horse and wasted no time in getting into the saddle. With Ki at her side, they rode past the governor's mansion on Colorado Street, and they could see the state capitol building being constructed out of red granite rock. It was going to be impressive, if they ever got it finished. Jessie guessed that construction had been going on for over five years, and there still seemed plenty to do. Captain Ray lived out near Shoal Creek, and it took them less than fifteen minutes to reach the man's big adobe house.

They dismounted and went to the the door and banged on it loudly using a blacksmith's hammer that was hanging by a leather thong. "The cap'n has always been a little deaf," Jessie said.

"That's because he's shot too many guns and rifles," Ki told her.

"What has that got to do with it?"

"Loud noises destroy the hearing," Ki explained. "That's another reason why a samurai uses a bow and arrows, *shuriken* blades, and his hands and feet as weapons."

Jessie said nothing. Actually, she had known men who had fired cannons who were totally deaf, but she'd never really put the cause and effect together. There might be something to what Ki was saying.

"Jessie!" the captain bellowed as he opened the door and scooped her up into his arms. "I'd about given up on you!"

"You know I'd have come even if I had to walk all the way from Circle Star."

He blushed with pleasure, and she was surprised to see he did not look sick at all. The Ranger set Jessie down as gently as if she were made of crystal. "You get more beautiful every time I see you, Jessie. If I was thirty...no, make that forty years younger, I'd move heaven and earth to sweep you off your feet."

He stepped back and extended his paw to Ki. And though he was old and a little bent, with liver spots on his face and hands, he still had a powerful grip. Captain Ray had stood an even six feet and the legends said he had once possessed the strength of a giant. "Good to see you, Ki. Have you been doing your job and taking care of our girl?"

Ki started to say something about the Beesleys, but Jessie cut him off. They had gotten tricked and almost killed, but that was in the past and there was no need to upset the old Ranger with an unpleasant story. "He's always keeping me out of trouble, Ben. With Ki around, danger runs from me and life gets mighty monotonous at times."

Ben led them into the adobe. It was cool, spacious, and cluttered with a lifetime of memorabilia celebrating his lifelong career with the Texas Rangers. In fact, every time that Jessie entered this home she had the feeling that it was a composite of the history of Texas. There was the Lone Star flag that had flown over the defeated Mexico City. One of Sam Colt's original six-shot revolvers was prominently displayed, along with Sam Walker's picture and some of the drawings he'd taken back East in order to show Colt what modifications were needed to market the gun successfully along the western frontier.

There were Mexican sabers taken from the Battle of Guadalupe Hidalgo, and hundreds of other artifacts including one of General Santa Anna's own silver inlaid pistols.

Captain Ray loved to show off his treasures. He said, "My only regret is that I never was able to find the son of a bitch that has Jim Bowie's knife. They musta taken if off his body when he died at the Alamo. And the Mexican who owns it now could sell it for a fortune in Texas."

"Yes," Jessie said, "but he'd never live to spend a cent

29

of the money. He'd be riddled by bullets before he ever reached the Rio Grande."

Ben chuckled. "That he would, darlin', that he would. Would you care for something to drink?"

Jessie shook her head as she pulled out the Ranger's letter. "I'd like to get right to the problem," she said.

Captain Ray's smile faded and he nodded solemnly. "All right. Sit down and I'll tell you everything. But I'm not a bit sure that you can help."

Jessie said nothing. She and Ki just waited for the old man to begin, and it seemed to take him quite a while to fix a beginning. "Outside of the late Sam Houston, do you know who I admire most in this world?"

Jessie was in no mood for guessing games, but she decided to play along with this one. Old Ben Ray was not a man to be rushed. "No."

"Think hard. I'll give you a hint," Ben said, filling and then lighting his pipe before saying another word. "He's a Texas legend and a hero and still acting as a captain in the Ranger force."

"Captain Semus Jones," Jessie said without hesitation.

Ben got his pipe going good and he looked pleased. "That's right. Old Semus was once under me and we were stationed in Del Rio. Did I ever tell you about the time we rode north and the two of us ran smack into a war party of Comanche?"

"I don't believe you have." Jessie winked at Ki. They had both heard that particular story at least six times, and this would probably be the seventh. But Ben loved reminiscing so much that neither Jessie nor Ki had the heart to rob him of the pleasure he derived from telling and retelling his favorite stories.

"Well, Semus had three pistols and I had two and we each had one old Sharps rifle. All single shots, of course."

"Of course," Jessie said.

"Well, Semus and I jumped down from our horses, and that was the first thing we did that those Injuns didn't expect. They thought we'd run, but instead we used our rifles and shot the chief. We both drilled him square and Semus, he was so damned mad that we'd wasted an unnecessary bullet on that Comanche chief, that he screamed bloody murder."

Ben laughed to himself. "Well, we jumped on our horses and charged those Indians, jest a-yellin' like the hounds of hell. We wasted no more bullets, and by the time we got among 'em we was swinging them Sharps rifles like clubs and knockin' Indians in every direction. Semus was a crazy man. He fought like he was possessed by the devil, and them Indians wanted no part of him. They put a spear into his side and he just pulled it out and drilled one of them plumb straight through the gizzard. Took all the piss and vinegar right outta them, and they ran. And there was still a good dozen!"

Ben closed his eyes almost as if he could see Semus and himself in action as they fought off a greatly superior force of Comanche. "We batted about half of 'em off the backs of their ponies before our own horses gave out. Then we reloaded and waited to see what would happen to them that got away."

"But they never came back," Ki said quietly. "They just left their dead and wounded and rode north, flying like the wind."

Ben frowned. "How'd you know?"

Jessie shot Ki a disapproving look, and the samurai said, "I guessed."

"Hummph! Well, that just happens to be the way it actually happened, Ki. Just the way it did. And if you needed proof, there's the Comanche war lance that Semus pulled out of his side and threw to the ground. For some reason, I wanted it real bad. He said I was a fool but he didn't say I couldn't take it, and so I picked it up and carried it all the way back down here to San Antonio. Still got Semus's dried blood on the blade. I'm going to give it to the Texas State Historical Society in my will along with all this other damned junk I got all over the place. They said they wanted every bit of it for . . . for posterity. That's what they called it."

Jessie nodded. "Ben. What kind of trouble made you send for us?"

His watery old eyes had been fixed on the Comanche war lance and its feathers. But now, he turned his attention back to Jessie. "I'm plumb ashamed to tell you, Jessie."

"We dropped out of my roundup and rode a long, hard trail to come and help you, Ben," Jessie said quietly. "Now that we're here, why don't you just lay it out on the table and let Ki and I decide if we can do anything or not. I've been going half crazy trying to figure out why a Texas Ranger like you wouldn't call upon the Rangers if he was in a tight fix."

Ben looked right at her. "Because," he said, almost at the level of a whisper, "what it is, is that everyone's starting to say that Captain Semus Jones and his boy—a Texas Ranger himself—are on the take and have both gone crooked as a pair of sidewinders. And if Captain Jones has gone bad, he might have taken half his men with him. It could be a real can of worms down in El Paso."

Jessie blinked. She knew Semus Jones, though not real well. Semus was fashioned from the exact same mold as Ben. His son, Gifford, was an exact duplicate of his famous father. Tall, ruggedly good-looking, and absolutely fearless. "Who's saying these things?"

Ben scrubbed his face. "Well, it started with a man

32

named Peterson who was transferred out of the El Paso office where Semus has been in charge for more than twenty years. He said that the Joneses, both father and son, were on the take from a rich Mexican rancher named Antonio Castillo. Castillo is known far and wide as a cattle rustler and slave smuggler. He has a small army he keeps in Juarez and uses them to raid across the border. He seems to lead a charmed life. He never makes the same mistake twice and he has the loyalty of all the Mexicans because he's generous to those who help him make money. The bastard is almost like a hero to those people."

"I've heard of him," Jessie said. "But I'd also heard that he was killed several years back down near Brownsville."

"Nope. We thought we had him, and there was a hell of a battle, but his body was never found, and he disappeared. Came back, though. If I could sit a horse and ride into Mexico like I used to do, I'd go after him and international borders be damned."

Jessie smiled. "They never stopped you before."

"Well," Ben said, conceding the point, "things have changed a little bit since we signed the big treaty. Our government frowns on the Texas Rangers crossing the border and killing or hanging Mexican bandits. Our boys still ride across the border and bring back stolen stock. But they better have a brand on their rump or a Ranger will get his own tail chewed good."

"You said Castillo deals in slaves as well as horses and cattle. White slaves?"

"Any color slaves. He's been known to steal a few Comanche and Kiowa women and sell them at the markets in Mexico City. But mostly it's settler women. Girls, when he or his men can grab 'em. We know he also deals with the Comancheros. They're all tied up in it together. Nasty business, that."

33

Jessie shivered. "Nasty business" was a real understatement. "What proof do the accusers have besides seeing the Jones men with Antonio Castillo?"

"I can't tell you, Jessie."

She frowned. "Why not?"

"Because if I told you, it couldn't help but make you think that old Captain Jones and Giff Jones are guilty as sin. I want you to go to El Paso without any preconceived notions in your pretty head. You and Ki will have to figure out a way to dig up your own evidence. Just be damned careful that there aren't a bunch of them in on it and get yourselves killed. What you have to do is ride with them if you can."

"How are we supposed to do that?" Ki asked. "The moment we arrive in town, Captain Jones is going to smell a trap. He'll know you sent us."

"Course he will. And I know that will make things a lot tougher for both of you, but it can't be helped. You're not Texas Rangers, but you still know how to dig around and sift through the bullshit to find the truth."

"What if Captain Jones *is* guilty?" Jessie asked, knowing how much it would hurt this man.

"Then I'd want him shot before he could be brought to trial, discrediting not only his own name but that of the Texas Rangers."

"And his son?"

"Same deal for Giff and any others that might have gone rotten," the old Ranger growled. "You give 'em the choice of killing themselves or having it done by one of us. The Texas Rangers clean their own house, Jessie. It hasn't happened in a long time but we'll do 'er if it has to be done."

Jessie expelled a deep breath. "I don't like this already," she admitted. "Legends die hard."

"Yeah, and they live hard, too," Ben said. "I'm not

34

asking you to whitewash anything, or to kill any Texas Ranger if they're guilty. Just get the message back to me. If you say they're guilty, then I'll know it's true and we'll do the rest."

Jessie shook her head. "You boys never have believed real strong in taking prisoners and bringing them to court."

"Rope justice or gun justice is the best," the old man said. "Always was, always will be."

Jessie glanced at Ki to signal that this discussion was ended unless he had any more questions. The samurai did not.

The Ranger captain relaxed. It was clear that he was relieved that the subject was over and he wanted it to be forgotten, at least for the evening. "Jessie," he said, "I've got a new Mexican cook named Pedro Garcia who makes the finest chili *verde* you ever tasted. He's making some up now with them big red peppers your father loved so much."

"Too hot for me," Jessie said, with a shake of her head.

"Me too," Ki added.

The old Ranger looked disgusted. "Well, dammit, anyway! How about some stew and biscuits, then?"

"That would be fine."

"Good," Ben said. "I'll have him warm up the stew for you sissies and I'll eat the chili *verde* myself. Play hell on my digestion, but even an old man has to live dangerously once in a while. Ain't that right?"

Jessie laughed. "I wouldn't know about that."

Ben grinned, but in his eyes Jessie saw sadness and worry. Today they would pretend as if everything was fine; but tomorrow she and Ki would be riding into an El Paso hornet's nest.

Chapter 4

Jessie and Ki arrived in El Paso the following week, hot, tired, and glad to be off the baking desert plains. El Paso was a city rich in history; as they rode up its dusty main street, Jessie was reminded how in the sixteenth century, Spaniards, trekking northward through the blistering deserts of Chihuahua, finally arrived here to refresh themselves at the waters of the Rio Grande. Two prominent mountain ranges rose steeply off the desert floor, divided by a pass. Because of it, those first Spanish explorers named this location *El Paso del Norte*—"the Northern Pass." Over the next several hundred years, a settlement had grown along both sides of the Rio Grande. Now, El Paso was overshadowed by the larger Mexican town of Cuidad Juarez, where thousands of Mexican families made their homes and worked in the fields and shops.

El Paso had always been a hard and dangerous town. The winds were constant and dust, heat, snakes, and scorpions were a fact of life. But the soil, irrigated by the warm Rio Grande, proved wonderfully fertile and there were many orchards and cultivated fields. There were immense cattle ranches in this country but the Apache, Comancheros, and Mexican *banditos* were a constant threat. They did not prey so much upon the wealthy ranchers as they did upon the peons who labored along both sides of the border. El Paso, like old Santa Fe, was a melting pot of two diverse cultures and an important staging point for trade. As it was dominated by its Spanish heritage and dependent upon the Mexican workers for cheap labor, a visitor to El Paso might be surprised to find that he was far more likely to hear Spanish than English spoken on the streets.

"Can you tell me where to find the Texas Ranger headquarters?" Jessie asked a man who was crossing the street with his head bowed into the wind and his hand on his hat to keep it from sailing away.

The man did not even look up, but he did point down the street. Feeling grit in her eyes and mouth, Jessie rode on down to the nearest livery. She passed the Ranger headquarters, having decided that she and Ki ought to take care of their horses and get them out of the wind and flying gravel before taking refuge themselves.

"Be two bits an animal per day," a fat, congenial man in his fifties said, holding out his chubby hand for the money. "Good looking horses like that, they ought to be grained and curried every day, too."

"How much extra?"

"Another two bits, miss. The grain is of better quality than the hay I got right now. Be a good idea to pay the extra money."

Jessie nodded and gave him five dollars. "Where's the best hotel in town?"

"Parker House, about ten doors down on the right. Can't miss it. You and the tall Chinaman here for business or pleasure?"

Ki stepped between them. "That's really none of your business, is it?"

The liveryman swallowed nervously. "No sir! Sure isn't. Now, you folks have a pleasant stay in El Paso. Don't worry none about these fine horses. They'll get the best care. And if you'd like those fine saddles of yours cleaned and oiled, that'll only cost . . ."

Jessie didn't even bother to answer. She pushed out of the livery into the hard, gritty wind and, lowering her head, she marched forward with her saddlebags. "Let's get a couple of hotel rooms before we go see Captain Jones and his men," she shouted.

Ki nodded. He did not like El Paso. It was so dry that it made the Circle Star ranch country seem like a tropical oasis. As far as he was concerned, the sooner that they could get this unpleasant and potentially very dangerous work over and done with, the happier he would be.

An hour later, Jessie and Ki emerged from their hotel and moved on down the boardwalk to the Ranger headquarters. It was small and cramped, with four desks and not a single Texas Ranger in sight. Its only occupant was an old man who was sitting behind a desk with a nameplate on it that read CAPTAIN SEMUS JONES, TEXAS RANGER.

"Howdy!" the old man chirped, popping his feet off the captain's desktop and bouncing to attention. "Can I help you folks with something?"

"We came to see the captain."

"Well, as you can see, he's gone. Been gone almost a week now."

"Where to?" Ki asked.

"Somewhere. I dunno. Them boys never tell me nothin'. They don't know nothin', either. They just hear of some trouble and away they ride."

"Where did they hear of trouble this time?" Jessie asked.

"There was some Apache raiding to the northwest of here, a hundred miles or so. Something about a few women being taken."

"That would be in New Mexico," Jessie said. "Do Texas Rangers ride into New Mexico?"

"They ride any damn place they want," the old man said. "Besides, the women could have been Texans. I dunno. I just hold things together for two bits a day. I dunno nothin' about nothin' 'cept I wouldn't be a Texas Ranger for all the gold in Montezuma's Mine. Damn rotten job. I was a butcher myself. I liked it. I could butcher a buffalo or a cow and have it hangin' on a hook before you could work up a spit."

Jessie shook her head. "I'll just bet you could, old timer." She reached into her Levi's and pulled out a dollar. "Why don't you go have a drink or two and enjoy yourself? I'm a friend of Captain Jones's. We'll watch the shop for an hour until you come back."

But the old man surprised Jessie when he shook his head. "No, miss. I couldn't rightly do that. The one order I got from the cap'n is never to leave anyone alone in here. They might do something they weren't supposed to do and then I'd lose my job. Pays right well, too, for doin' nothing but readin' and nappin'."

Jessie knew that it would be futile to try and pressure the old man into leaving. What she wanted—and needed —was a chance to poke around in Captain Jones's files and desk drawers. Not that she even knew what she was looking for, but it was a start.

"You're right," Jessie said, giving the old coot a warm smile. "I'll come back tomorrow morning and see if they've returned."

"Might easy be another week," the old man said. "Could be as long as a month. That was the longest time. Down in Mexico, they were. Aren't supposed to go down there, but they did, and I figured that the cap'n and Ranger Giff were goners for sure. We all thought they were

40

goners. But they came back good as new. Yes, sir! That man and his boy are a pair of ring-tailed fighters."

"Did they ever say where they were in Mexico?"

"Nope. Cap'n Jones, he never talks much about where he goes or what he does. He's damn near as old as me, but you'd never know it by looking at him. He shoots straight, has good hearing, and is steady. Gets drunk same as his men, and nobody ever makes the mistake of crossing him. They know that even if they should kill the cap'n, Giff or one of the others would kill them."

Jessie and Ki went back to their hotel rooms. That evening, they had dinner in the hotel restaurant—the usual steaks, potatoes, and apple pie, but very good. "What we need to do," Jessie said over her after-dinner coffee, "is to get back into that Ranger headquarters tonight and see what we can find."

"That shouldn't be too hard," Ki said. "Why don't you let me do this alone?"

"Uh-uh. I know you're a ninja and I'll make the risks greater for you, but I want to have a look for myself."

Ki had also finished his meal and now was sitting very relaxed in his chair. "Do you really think that a Texas Ranger would actually leave some kind of incriminating evidence just lying around in his files or in his desk?"

"I don't know. I kind of suspect that a Texas Ranger headquarters has never been broken into before. And if the whole office is involved with Señor Castillo, then we might actually find something of value."

"Not likely," Ki said. "And I hope these so-called 'rumors' of corruption prove groundless."

"So do I," Jessie said. "The Texas Ranger tradition is something that means a lot in this country. It only takes one bad apple to spoil all the work that they've done in protecting the frontier."

She finished her coffee. "If you're ready to go, then so am I," she told the samurai. "Let's meet at midnight."

The moon shone brightly and the stars were brilliant as Jessie and Ki moved to the rear of the building and tried the back door. "It has a strong dead-bolt locked from inside," Ki said, after several minutes. "I think we're going to have to go in either through the front door or the window."

Jessie kept glancing up and down the back alley and wishing that the moon was not quite so full. "It's your decision," she said.

Ki slipped along the side of the building. When he came to the front street, he eased around the corner of the building and studied the street. He was dismayed to note that there were still quite a few people out on this hot summer night, and he wondered if he and Jessie should try again in about three hours. But he knew Jessie was very weary from their long ride and he very much wanted her to get at least half a night's rest.

Ki moved to the front door and tested the lock. He found that it was vulnerable to a pick, and he removed one from his sleeve. He was not expert at this sort of thing but he worked steadily until he heard it click.

"Come on," he whispered, removing the lock and grabbing the door-handle. He pushed inside, Jessie right on his heels.

Because they had been in the Ranger headquarters less than ten hours before, they had little trouble going right to Captain Jones's desk. "Light a candle and let's take a peek," Jessie said, reaching for the middle desk drawer.

Ki had brought both candles and matches, and now he lit one. "I'd better keep it down low. There are no window shades or curtains on that big front window," he said.

Jessie's hand was sliding open the drawer as she turned to glance at the window. "Yes, that—"

The explosion blew out the front of the drawer and knocked her down. Jessie felt a sharp pain in her left hand. She tasted gunpowder and smoke as she struck the floor. "Ki," she whispered weakly as she began to lose consciousness. "We have to get out of here!"

The samurai had been half turned toward the front window when the double-barreled shotgun that had been rigged to fire went off. The explosion had caught him completely off guard and he dropped the candle. As it sputtered into extinction, Ki could see the twin smoking barrels protruding from where the front of the desk drawer had been. "Jessie!"

His fingers touched the soft hollow of her throat. She was alive, but as the candle went out, he could not tell how badly she had been shot. He scooped her up in his arms and charged the front door. The loud shotgun blast would bring the curious running, and he did not want to be caught and made to answer questions.

Ducking into the side alley, he ran with a sense of panic that threatened to overwhelm him. When he had put some distance between himself and the Ranger headquarters, he stopped and eased Jessie down on the dirt. There was enough moonlight to show that she had not been seriously injured. The samurai was almost overcome with relief. Had she been standing directly in front of Captain Jones's rigged-up desk, the double shotgun blast would have cut her in half.

"Legend or not," Ki vowed through teeth clenched in anger, "when I find Captain Jones, I'm going to have a few words to say!"

Jessie had regained consciousness. She supposed she had fainted from the effects of the lancing pain and the sudden shock of the impact. She expected to see her hand mangled, but was relieved to see that only a few pellets had struck her and that she still had all her fingers intact on her left hand, though her thumb was badly torn. "I'm all right now," she said, trying to keep her voice calm.

"I had better find a doctor," Ki said.

Jessie climbed a little unsteadily to her feet with Ki's assistance. "We'll get the hand cleaned up in my room. I trust myself to bandage it better than some doctor would at this hour." She shook her head. She knew that she was incredibly lucky just to be alive. "I just don't understand why Captain Jones would have done something like that while he was away."

"There's only one possible explanation," Ki snapped, furious at himself for allowing any of Jessie's blood to be spilled. "The captain has something to hide. Something that he feels strong enough about to kill in order to protect."

"It doesn't look very good for him, does it?" Jessie said.

"No."

They managed to get up the back steps of the hotel and to her room without incident. "It's barely a scratch," Jessie said, dipping her injured left hand in a cool washbowl of water and rinsing the blood away. "I'll be just fine."

But the samurai took the hand and inspected it closely. "It needs a doctor to look at it in the morning, Jessie."

"If I do that he'll know I was there. There is no way that I can see a doctor in this town."

"Then we can find one in Juarez," Ki said.

Jessie realized that the samurai was right. The thumb was pretty mangled and it needed stitching. Already, the bandages she had just applied were sopped with blood. Jessie gripped the thumb and applied hard pressure. "Okay," she said. "We'll find a doctor in Juarez. And while we're down there, we might as well take the opportunity to pay a visit to Señor Antonio Castillo."

Ki's eyes widened a fraction. "You mean, just like that?"

"Yes. Just like that. We can pose as buyers of cattle or slaves."

"What if the man recognizes you as one of the richest women in the world?"

Jessie didn't have an answer to that question. So far, she and Ki had made one mistake after another since leaving Circle Star. It was about time that their luck turned and they did something right. "We'll take that risk," she said with determination. "We've come too far to miss turning over any stone in this investigation. This Señor Castillo could be the answer to everything. I want to see if I can bend him to my will."

Ki said nothing, but he did not approve. He would much rather have gone after the Texas Rangers, starting with the captain himself. But the samurai was at Jessie's command and he would never question her authority. Ki was not a servant, but neither was he the kind of man to remain quiet if he thought wise counsel was necessary. "What man could resist your will?" he asked quietly.

Jessie looked up from her injured thumb. "Right now," she said, "almost any man."

Chapter 5

They splashed their horses across the shallow Rio Grande late the next afternoon and entered Mexico. It was not much different from Texas—maybe a little poorer looking, but except for the fact that the Rio Grande was an international border, there was no distinction between Juarez and El Paso. Children with round, curious eyes watched them ride by, and dogs with their ribs showing and their tails wagging barked in their passing. Jessie saw señoritas in gaily colored dresses working beside their mothers, cooking and cleaning. An old man led his burro, laden with firewood, past them, and a handsome young *vaquero* came galloping past on a fine sorrel horse. His clothes were braided with gold and his saddle had pieces of silver on it. He touched the brim of his wide sombrero and flashed Jessie a dazzling smile. Jessie nodded, her eyes glowing with approval, for he was devilishly handsome. She had always admired the *vaqueros,* and employed many of them on Circle Star. Superb horsemen, without equal when it came to the reata, they were fun loving, dashing, and yet incredibly loyal when well treated and respected.

Ki glanced sideways at her. "It's remarkable how quickly you have recovered from our long ride and last night's near disaster."

"I slept a solid ten hours last night—and in a feather bed, no less. I feel much better, except for the thumb."

Ki frowned and studied the heavily bandaged append-age. "Is it still bleeding?"

"Yes, but only a little."

Ki reined his horse in and dismounted. He walked over to a woman working and said, *"Por favor, señora.* Uhh . . . doctor?"

The woman stared at him with incomprehension. Ki frowned. He glanced at Jessie and pointed to her bandaged thumb. "Doctor? *Sí?"*

The woman still did not respond. Ki grew impatient. He pulled out his *tanto* knife and made slashing motions at his thumb and added a very pained expression. The Mexican woman was beginning to become alarmed. Jessie's own Spanish was not good, but she did know the word for doctor. *"Por favor, señora. Médico?"*

Now the woman understood. *"Sí! Sí!"* she cried, point-ing up the street while talking a mile a minute. Jessie had to slow her down and it took several minutes before she understood that there was a doctor named Emilio Sanchez six doors down the crowded street.

"Gracias, señora," Jessie said, riding on past the smil-ing woman.

Dr. Sanchez was a short, chubby young man with spar-kling eyes and incredibly white teeth which he flashed often. Fortunately, he spoke a little English. He unwound Jessie's bandaged thumb as if it were a fragile glass sculp-ture and he made a huge fuss over the wounds. He asked Jessie how she received such a terrible injury and Jessie pretended not to understand the question. Sanchez dropped that line of questioning and studied the thumb from every conceivable angle, though Jessie suspected he was looking at a whole lot more than her thumb while he fiddled and fussed around. Despite his rather amorous behavior, it comforted her to see that the young doctor's office was clean and an already yellowing diploma from some college in Mexico City was framed and hanging on his wall. There were a lot of American doctors practicing on the frontier who had never seen a medical college and who had learned everything they knew by trial and error. Such men were always to be avoided.

Dr. Sanchez did prove to be competent. After studying the injury as long as he dared, all the while hinting that he would like to do a few "follow-up house calls," he gave Jessie a water glass full of tequila. When she was slightly tipsy, he did a quick suture job, surprisingly expert, considering that the samurai was hanging over his shoulder watching every single move. He gave her some herbs to boil every day and soak the thumb in and then he touched her face and said, *"One hundred pesos, señorita, or . . . perhaps . . ."*

He looked right at Jessie and winked; then his sparkling eyes slid down to admire the swell of her breasts. Jessie almost threw her head back and laughed. She paid the doctor and could not help but notice that Ki had not found the doctor's attentions all that amusing. Jessie sometimes wondered if Ki were not a little jealous. Oh, sure, he was like her brother, but when men gawked at her or made advances, the samurai was as likely as not to become slightly irritable.

"Thank you, Señor Sanchez. Now, could you tell me where I can find a Señor Antonio Castillo?"

Sanchez had been grinning hugely. He had a rather large, hooked nose and a small, bushy mustache. He was cute. But now he suddenly seemed worried and acted as if he had been thrown completely off his guard. "Señor Castillo?"

"Sí."

The doctor shrugged his narrow shoulders and marched stiffly over to a window. "There," he said. "Casa Castillo."

Jessie could not imagine how she and Ki could have missed it, for it sat alone on a low hill. It was surrounded by an adobe wall about twelve feet tall, and, even though it was about a quarter of a mile beyond the outskirts of Juarez, it was clear that the *Casa* was almost like a fortress. *But then,* Jessie asked herself, *what should I have expected?*

"It is dangerous, *señorita,*" the doctor warned before he turned away.

"*Sí,*" Jessie said, her eyes still resting on the fortress. "Thank you."

The doctor nodded, but he did not turn around and his smile for her was gone. Jessie thought that he must be assuming that she was either Castillo's woman, or a slave, or else a very expensive prostitute imported across the border. In any case, he made it very obvious that he wanted nothing to do with a woman associated with Señor Castillo. His behavior and demeanor had changed completely. He was curt and all business as he took her money and showed them the door.

"You sure dampened his ardor," Ki said as they left the doctor's office "This Castillo must really have a bad reputation, even south of the border. I want to go in alone and have a meeting with the man. If that doesn't work, you can go."

Jessie shook her head. "Let's try it the other way. I go in first and you follow."

"That's the worst idea I've ever heard," Ki said.

"All right, then we both go in, but not together. I think that it would be better if Castillo doesn't realize that we are a team."

"That makes sense," Ki said. "That way, if he simply

has one of his lieutenants shoot one of us, the other can shoot him."

Jessie shook her head. "Not funny."

"Neither was the little doctor who propositioned you," Ki said. "Shall we go and meet the rich and famous Castillo?"

"Let's go." Jessie took a deep breath. "I just hope we don't find a Texas Ranger by the name of Semus Jones."

"The old man said they were chasing Indians in New Mexico Territory," Ki said.

"That's right," Jessie said. "But we didn't believe him at the time, and I see no reason to believe that now. What better excuse to disappear for a week or two into Juarez and Castillo's web of evil?"

"I agree," Ki said.

Jessie had to admit that she felt butterflies in her stomach as she rode up the hill on Sun to see if she could arrange a meeting with Señor Castillo. It was possible that Castillo might have seen her somewhere, or the description of her beauty might have preceded her. But then, even if Castillo did realize who she was, she could still bluff her way into his good graces by fabricating some story about how she had come down to buy some stolen cattle or horses. Castillo was nothing but a rich and talented *bandito*. He needed buyers, or he would be out of business. Jessie felt sure that she could convince him of her sincerity and perhaps even gain his confidence enough to learn about the Texas Rangers.

If there was going to be a problem, it rested in how to find out what she needed to know and then to get out of Juarez without being forced to compromise herself in Castillo's arms. Jessie was aware of the effect she had on men. Castillo was probably a man accustomed to having his choice of any woman he wanted, whenever he wanted. He

51

would, of course, have that Latin machismo; coupled with his unbridled power, the combination was quite likely to demand a bedroom conquest.

Jessie was glad that Ki would also be coming into Castillo's stronghold. She had assumed that the entrance to the fortress would be guarded. If she could, she would make sure she created a small but important diversion for the samurai. But even if that were not possible, there was no fortress in the world that could keep a *ninja* from entering whenever he desired. Ki would simply wait until darkness and then slip past the guards or scale the fortress walls as easily as a child at play. And he would find her; Jessie knew that he would. He would come, and, if things got out of hand with Castillo, he would be there as swiftly as a ray of light piercing the darkness.

Even so as she approached the gateway to the Castillo fortress, Jessie had to admit to some apprehensions. So many things could go wrong—and had already gone wrong. And as far as Captain Semus Jones was concerned, she had ridden into El Paso believing that the man was innocent until proven guilty. But after having her hand nearly shot off by a sawed-off shotgun cleverly rigged to fire when a desk drawer was pulled, Jessie was not so certain about Captain Jones anymore. Honest men did not set deadly traps.

Two guards jumped out from cover and, with rifles at their shoulders, shouted, *"Alto!"*

Jessie knew that the word meant "halt," and she wasted no time in pulling Sun to a stop. The men approached cautiously until they saw that underneath the wide Stetson hat was a young woman. They quickly lowered their rifles and gazed at her with real interest. They began to ask questions so rapidly that Jessie could not begin to translate. *"No hablo español!"*

She dismounted, the top two buttons of her blouse undone to show some cleavage. The guards looked at each other and then back at Jessie, who removed her hat and shook down her long, reddish-blond hair. The guards licked their lips and Jessie smiled and walked straight up to them. *"Señor Castillo?"*

They were unable to hide their disappointment, but they tried. Nodding their heads up and down, they escorted her toward an immense two-storied house that had balconies on both floors. She halted at the door. As she tied Sun to a hitching post, she glanced quickly toward the gate just in time to see the shadow of the samurai pass through it and then vanish along the wall. Ki's presence filled her with hope, and she waited as one of the guards disappeared into the house.

It seemed to take forever before a lean and hawk-faced man in his thirties came out to see Jessie. He studied her carefully and then he said in English, "Who are you and what do you want?"

Jessie was taken aback by his brusqueness but relieved that the man spoke such good English. She smiled. "I wish to see Señor Castillo."

"For what reason?"

His expression did not soften, nor did the slightest hint of warmth creep into his voice. Jessie dropped her smile, knowing this was one of those rare men who could not be charmed. He had the look of a wolf and a ravager of women. There was no romance or humor in his eyes, which were black and dead in the orbits of his bony face.

"I come to talk business."

"You want something from Señor Castillo. What is it?"

Jessie found herself disliking this man very much and losing her patience. "That is for him to know, señor. Not you. Tell him Señora Starr is here to see him."

53

The man did not like being told what to do. "Does he expect you?"

Jessie raised her chin and gambled. "Yes. Tell him I have come far to meet him and I will not be turned away."

For the first time, the man relaxed a little. "I can tell by looking at you that you will be in his bed before sundown. But it is my responsibility to know what price you ask. Don Antonio is a very rich man, no? You come here for his money."

"I have some money of my own. What I come for is my own and Don Castillo's business. Please take me to him at once."

The man's lips curled. "You are too quick to give the orders. But this time, I will take you as you wish. Come!"

Without waiting for her, he turned on his heel and marched imperiously back through the heavy oak doors from which he had emerged. Jessie followed, her mind racing. He had said that she would be in Castillo's bed before sundown. Hellfire! Sundown was less than two hours from now. This man must be a fast worker.

Jessie was led into a courtyard of great beauty. There was a huge fountain, half covered with floating water-lilies that shaded brightly colored fish. Flowers whose names she did not know hung from every branch of every tree in a wild profusion of colors. The courtyard was surrounded on two sides by the *casa* itself and on the other two by another twelve-foot wall covered with honeysuckle. It seemed twenty degrees cooler than out in the streets of Juarez, and jasmine filled the air like perfume. After traveling hundreds of miles across the parched plains of West Texas, then seeing the dust, filth, and hard life of El Paso and Juarez, this courtyard seemed like a paradise.

"Be seated, Señora Starr," the man commanded. "I will

ask Don Antonio if he wishes to honor you with his presence."

Jessie said nothing. It was clear that the man was possessive and highly suspicious of her but that was to be expected. Jessie smoothed the creases of her riding habit. She discreetly rebuttoned the second button on her blouse and glanced into the fountain but could not see her reflection. She hoped she did not look either too inviting or too trail-weary. She had already decided to pose as an American cattle rancher's widow, who had come from around Houston and who was desperate to buy cheap stolen herds of longhorn cattle. It wasn't a great story, but maybe it was just off-beat enough so that this man would be inclined to believe her. Besides, Houston was over six hundred miles across almost the entire breadth of her Lone Star state, and it was very unlikely that a man of Castillo's reputation would dare to travel such a distance across American territory protected by Texas Rangers. To do so would be to put his life in great jeopardy.

"Buenas tardes, señora!" he said, in a deep, cultured voice. "Rodrigo Lopez did not warn me that you were so beautiful."

Jessie turned to see a dapper, handsome man in his forties bow slightly and reach for her hand. She gave it to him and he kissed it, his mustache actually tickling her a little. When he straightened, she saw that his eyes were not black but dark blue, and she knew at once that he was of Spanish blood with very little Indian in his heritage. Dressed in a black coat and trousers with fancy embroidery work and wearing a white silk shirt and red scarf, he was a real dandy.

"Good evening, Don Castillo. My name is Jessica Starr."

She was looking right into his eyes and saw nothing of

recognition or alarm. Reassured, she pressed on. "I have come in the hope of doing business with you."

"So Rodrigo Lopez tells me. But please, let us not talk business so quickly. You have come a long way?"

"Yes, from north of Houston. I own a cattle ranch. Nothing too big, but big enough."

"And its name?"

"One Star," Jessie said quickly, angry at herself for not having anticipated such an obvious question. "It was left to me by my late husband, Señor Kendal Starr. Perhaps you have heard of him?"

"I'm afraid not. But I must extend my deepest sympathies for your late husband. To have left one so beautiful as yourself is a tragedy of major proportions."

"He was old and tired," Jessie said, warming up to the story and deciding that the more off-beat it sounded, the more likely it was to be believed. "He and my father were early ranchers. He was like an uncle, but then . . . well, he needed a wife and I needed his strength."

"But it must have taken great strength to come here alone. Rodrigo says you are alone. Is that not true?"

"It is. I have a . . . a friend but I insisted he remain in El Paso until I had spoken to you."

Castillo clapped his hands together sharply and very suddenly. "We must have some refreshments. At once! You must stay the night, and we can talk business perhaps tomorrow or the next day. Eh?"

There could be no doubt as to what he really wanted to talk about between now and tomorrow morning. The man's hot blue eyes almost sizzled. "Perhaps," Jessie said quietly as a pitcher of something cold and delicious was brought out to them by a pretty young girl in her teens. The girl looked at Castillo with worry and then at Jessie with smoldering hatred. Jessie knew at once that the girl was jealous

56

and that she was this man's lover. He was old enough to be her father, but he was definitely her lover.

"Go, Anita!" Castillo commanded the girl with a wave of his hand. "Leave us to talk."

The girl stomped off, and Jessie could not help but pity her. She was at the height of her bloom, but even now she had no hold on this man. And in a few years she would begin to wilt and probably be passed along to Castillo's lieutenants before eventually winding up with the lowest of his soldiers. By then, a man like Castillo would have sullied four or five more girls and robbed them of their honor and dignity. Such was the way of a rich Mexican who dealt in slavery and stolen livestock down in a poor country.

"I really must talk with you," Jessie said. "About cattle. You see, I had to sell off my own herds in order to satisfy some of my husband's debts. So now I have the land, the grass, and the water, but no cattle and no money to buy them at current Houston market prices."

"What are they bringing in Houston?"

"Five dollars a head. And I can run at least ten thousand head."

Even Don Castillo was impressed. He lifted his glass in salute and said, "To tall grass and beautiful women."

Jessie drank to that. The liquid was delicious but it had a very warm taste to it as it slid down her throat. "What is this?"

"Tequila and a very special mix that women seem to enjoy."

"It's delicious." And it was. Jessie drank some more and Don Antonio refilled her glass and his own as well. That was comforting, because Jessie would not have put it past him to try and drug her.

"How much would you pay for these cattle?" he asked.

"Delivered to the border . . . say at Guadalupe de Bravo, a few miles south of here."

"You could do that?"

He chuckled and said, "Certainly. All you have to do is to ask. And pay, of course."

Jessie was enjoying this more than she had expected. "How much, Don Antonio?"

"Because you are so beautiful and we are going to be friends, three dollars a head."

"Two dollars."

He again raised his glass. "Two dollars and a half and we have finished our business and can speak of pleasure, no?"

Jessie knew when to pull up the slack. "It's a deal, providing the cattle are unbranded and healthy . . . and . . . that you can keep the Texas Rangers from knowing about this. With ten thousand cattle coming out of Mexico, someone is almost sure to hear of it and perhaps go to Ranger headquarters seeking a reward."

Castillo looked into her eyes and smiled. "That is not your worry, but mine," he said. "There are always ways to take care of such problems."

"With the Texas Rangers?" Jessie asked, making sure that her skepticism was not missed.

"Even with them," Castillo assured her in that smooth, rich voice of his. "They are not gods, though your people would like to believe otherwise. They are just men. And men are always corruptible. A man cannot live off tradition or a tin star. He must have money and . . . other things. Sometimes beautiful things, sometimes things that pleasure him in the deepest hour of the night."

Jessie felt sick. So there were Texas Rangers on the take and in the corrupt hands of this clutching man. The rumors were all true. She reached out and took her drink in her hand and then emptied it quickly. She heard Don Castillo laugh confidently down deep in his throat, and she wanted to grab the pitcher of drinks and smash it into his face, ruining that smug handsomeness and defiling the immaculate image he presented. But instead, she leaned back in her chair and gazed like a sheep into his eyes.

Let him think that he had her. Let him step into her trap.

Chapter 6

The samurai had come to rest on the top of the adobe courtyard wall and had covered himself with honeysuckle. He had lain perfectly still for almost two hours listening to Jessie and Don Castillo talk and laugh. He had also seen Jessie pour most of her many drinks underneath their table to trickle through the tile stones and seep into the ground. Don Castillo, however, was getting bolder as he drank. He had tried to move next to Jessie and put his arm around her waist, but she had blocked his advance and kept him at arm's distance. But sooner or later, probably after dinner, Don Castillo would be unwilling to wait any longer. He would insist that Jessie come to his bedroom. It was then that Ki intended to strike. Don Castillo would be alone and, in the darkness of the room, he would be easy prey.

But to carry out his plan, Ki needed to locate Don Castillo's bedroom. This he was more than prepared to do as soon as darkness fell and the hallways of the magnificent *casa* grew dim.

"I'm quite hungry," Jessie said, her voice drifting up to the samurai. "Could we eat something, Don Castillo?"

Ki smiled. Jessie probably was hungry, for they had not eaten since leaving El Paso.

The rich Mexican outlaw touched Jessie's cheek. "I will feed you the fruit of love from my vine, little pet!"

Ki almost burst out laughing. Darkness had crept across the secluded courtyard, but servants had hung lanterns all around so that the samurai could see Jessie's outraged expression, see how she struggled magnificently not to slap the drunken fool who had dared to call Jessica Starbuck "little pet." Ki admired Jessie's restraint. It was good sometimes for her to have to test her self-control under the most adverse situations imaginable. Jessie was undergoing just such a test at this very moment and doing quite well. Ki was proud of her.

"But what I need is real food," Jessie managed to say. "Please, Don Castillo, love can not gush from a starving body!"

Ki covered his mouth and chortled silently. He would remember that line and use it someday on Jessie when she least expected it.

Castillo sighed very loudly. "As you wish," Castillo said, obviously realizing that as long as this woman was hungry for food she would not be willing to satisfy his own hungers. "We shall eat! Come with me to the dining room."

He stood up, keeping both hands flat on the table to steady himself. Jessie looked up and Ki waved down at her. She rolled her eyes and then flashed him a pained smile. "Let me take your arm," she said to the tottering Mexican.

Don Castillo nodded gratefully. He drew himself up very straight and raised his chin in a dignified posture. Extending the crook of his arm to Jessie, he stepped back from the table and burped slightly. "You drink magnificently," he said, in awe of the beautiful woman at his side. "I hope that you have as much capacity for lovemaking."

Jessie stiffened for a moment, but then she said sweetly, "The night is very young, Don Castillo. I know that you must set a wonderful table for your guests. I have heard this even in El Paso."

"You have?"

"Yes."

Castillo nodded. "It is true. I will have my servants prepare you a magnificent dinner, Señora! Magnificent!"

"I can hardly wait," Jessie said as she led the swaying Don Castillo into the cool dimness of the *casa*.

Ki moved as soon as the servants had cleared away the empty pitcher and glasses. He dropped lightly down to the colored tiles and then glided across the courtyard until he came to the house itself. He ducked his head inside, and then entered. To his right, he could hear Don Castillo talking loudly. To his left, the halls were empty. Ki turned that way. He moved down the hall, peering into rooms. He knew that Castillo's bedroom would most likely be on the upper floor where, in summer, he would get a breeze. Also, the view would be superior.

Rapid footsteps caught the samurai halfway between two rooms with no place to run. He froze in the dim, candlelit hallway, knowing that he was trapped. He flattened up against the smooth adobe wall and held his breath. Suddenly, Rodrigo Lopez rounded a corner. He was walking very quickly, his mind absorbed by his own thoughts, so that he did not see the samurai until it was too late.

The edge of Ki's hand was as hard as an axe handle, and as Rodrigo raised his head and a shout of warning filled his throat, Ki brought that hand down solidly against the base of the Mexican lieutenant's neck. The samurai could easily have broken the neck had he wanted, but he checked his leverage and power just a fraction so that when the stiff edge of his hand struck, it did not kill Rodrigo but only dropped him soundlessly to the floor.

Ki grabbed the man by the feet and dragged him down the hallway until he came to a room. He opened the door

63

and pulled him inside and was just closing the door behind him when a body came flying off a bed. Ki ducked at the last instant but he still felt a sharp and instant pain as a knife sliced along the side of his neck. Another inch to the side and he would certainly have had his throat slit.

Off balance and still trying to close the door so that the struggle did not arouse the entire household, Ki had all he could do to keep from being skewered. The door slammed shut, plunging the room into total darkness. Ki ducked and threw himself blindly at his attacker. He knew he had been fortunate enough to knock the knife spinning, for he heard it slide across the floor. And to his utter amazement and relief, his arms gripped a naked, very curvaceous woman.

"I keel you!" she shouted in heavily accented English. "What's the matter, the American woman turn you down, Antonio? You come to my bed again, Antonio? Never again!"

Ki pinned her to the floor. "I am not Don Antonio," he told the hellcat beneath him. "*I* am his enemy, too."

The woman stiffened with shock. She struggled like crazy to free herself but he pinioned her with his strong body. "Who are you? Don't scream, señorita, or I will silence you very quickly."

It was not an empty threat. Already, Ki's fingers had found an *atemi,* or pressure point, at the base of her throat. He had the skill to render her unconscious in an instant if she took a deep breath in anticipation of calling for help.

"I will not scream," she panted. "My name is Anita. Who are you?"

"Ki," he told her, seeing no point in hiding the truth.

"You say you are Antonio's enemy," she hissed. "Prove it and kill him!"

"Why? Because of your jealousy?"

"Yes! And also because I am doomed as his slave. Free me and I will . . . I will do anything."

Ki released her wrists. "I need to know where his bedroom is," he said.

Her laughter was not nice. "Oh," she whispered, "Anita knows his bedroom, all right. Only now, the gringo woman is probably already in his bed instead of me. And after her there will be many others. I was a fool to love him, I can see that now. Now, I want you to keel him and take me away from here."

"Tell me how to get to his bedroom."

Anita told him. He started to climb off of her, convinced that she really did hate Antonio Castillo and had not lied to him. But she clung to him tightly. "Not yet. Before you go, whoever you are, I want to do something for you so that you will come back for me when he is dead."

Before Ki could say anything, the young woman's hand slipped into the loose *ninja* trousers he wore. She took his manhood in her hand and kneaded it expertly with her fingers. "What difference does just a few minutes more make now, eh?"

Ki thought about it. He had not had a woman in weeks and had seen this one in the courtyard when Castillo had rudely dismissed her. She was quite pretty and obviously in need of some kind of retaliation toward Castillo. Ki decided that it would not be fair to deny her. He lifted up on his forearms and his lips found her breasts, first one, then the other. He sucked and teased them gently while she slid his pants off and brought him to full arousal.

"Oh, my stranger," she whispered in the darkness, "you are very big! Like a *caballo*—a horse!"

Ki smiled and his hand explored her soft, eager young body. His fingers trailed down between her legs and then into her nest of silky black hair. He slipped them into her womanhood and she moaned happily. "Wouldn't you rather get back in bed?" he asked.

"No, señor! Please. Do not stop doing it to me!"

Ki's long, supple fingers knew exactly how to arouse a woman. He brought her to the point where her buttocks were lifting off the floor as if trying to pull him into her. "Señor," she groaned, "have mercy, please!"

She was holding him with both hands now, pulling his manhood toward her hot cavern of desire with fierce urgency. Ki allowed her to do this, and, when the head of his throbbing rod touched her wet mass of hair, he slammed his hips forward and she cried out with a mixture of pain and pleasure. "Oh," she panted, "you are twice—no, three times—the man that Antonio is. Do not ever stop doing this to poor Anita. Never!"

Ki laughed softly from deep in his throat. He began to move his hips in a slow, excruciatingly pleasurable ellipse that quickly drove the Mexican girl to the point of distraction. She lifted her legs and locked her ankles together at the small of his back as he moved his hips faster and faster.

His lips clashed with hers, and when he felt her hard young body begin to buck and slam back at him, Ki covered her mouth with his own and drowned out her cries of hysterical gratification.

He could feel her heart pounding, and her breath was short, as if she had been running for miles. Ki stopped the circling movement and began to piston deeper than before, and more powerfully. "Now," he panted, "you shall have all of it!"

Anita swallowed. Her body twitching and her mind scattering like leaves in the wind, she could barely speak as he pounded in and out of her until they were both consumed by their passions and his great root erupted like a spewing geyser.

Jessie had eaten more than she should, in order to prolong the dinner until almost midnight. Castillo had also eaten very well and the food had sobered him up, but he was left irritable and impatient to satisfy his lust. Jessie knew that she could not stall the man much longer. She was determined, however, to learn whether or not Ranger Semus Jones was directly involved in cattle and horse rustling across the border.

"I will go with you," she said, studying the slightly drunken, increasingly belligerent man who sat across the dining table from her, "but first I must know this: I understand that there is a captain of the Texas Rangers, a man almost legendary in my state, who has many spies in Mexico. I cannot afford to take possession of stolen cattle, pay you thousands of dollars, and then have them confiscated by Captain Semus Jones. I must have concrete assurance that this man and his Rangers will not learn of this sale and then confiscate my cattle once they are across the Rio Grande River."

"You have nothing to worry about!" Castillo said in anger. "I have told you this."

Jessie decided that she could not allow this man to bully her. In an icy voice, she said, "Mere assurances mean nothing to me, Don Antonio. I want proof! Either that, or there is no deal."

He threw up his hands and shouted, "And what will finally satisfy you as proof? What must I do—invite Captain Jones here to sit with us and pledge that he will not arrest you and take your cattle?"

Jessie looked him right in the eye. "Yes, that would be good enough."

67

He stared at her with disbelief. His face was twisted with anger and flushed from the drinking. He looked old and terrible. "Then it shall be done!"

Jessie stared at him. Then her eyes dropped down to study the wine glass in her hand. She lifted it and the liquid rippled for her hands were shaking. "Then we have a deal, Don Antonio. And the business is finished."

"And the pleasure begins at last," he said, standing up and coming around to pull out her chair. He offered her his arm and led her out of the dining room. They walked down a long hallway lit by candles and then climbed a stairway. Another hallway and then they arrived at his bedroom. It was, she had to admit, rather impressive. Huge in size, there was a bed in the middle of it large enough for three men and women to couple with great intensity. There were weapons on the walls and a wardrobe that a king might have envied. The furniture was heavy and dark, imported from Spain or Italy. Bright red serapes served as rugs and curtains.

He wasted no time on pleasantries. He began to unbutton his shirt, and when he took it off she saw that he was sunken-chested and had little muscle. A round potbelly hung over his trousers. "Well?" he demanded of her.

Jessie lifted her skirt and removed a derringer from a rose-colored garter that belted her shapely thigh. When his jaw fell, she said, "Drop your trousers, Antonio, and I will blow your shriveled root all over the wall."

He went as white as a bedsheet. "Is this . . . is this some game?"

"No," she said, moving toward him. "This is very serious. And on second thought, I do want you to drop your pants right down to your ankles."

"*Por Diós!*" he cried. "Mercy! Don't shoot it off. Please!"

68

Jessie cocked the hammer back. "Now."

Castillo fumbled at his belt. He finally managed to get his pants unbuttoned and then down to his knees. He was wearing very colorful underpants.

"What are you going to do with me?"

"That," Jessie said, "is a very, very good question. I suppose it all depends on what you have to tell me about Captain Semus Jones, his son Gifford, and the rest of the Texas Rangers."

"I will tell you nothing!" he screeched. "If you shoot me, Rodrigo Lopez and my men will come running and you will die! Die on your back with an army of men—"

"Don't say another word!" Ki said, leaping into the room with Anita in tow. "Not one more word!"

Jessie looked at the samurai and then at the girl. "I see you were distracted. It doesn't matter. You came at the right moment. Captain Semus Jones is a traitor to his country and badge—"

At that moment, Castillo whirled, took two hops, and threw himself out the open second story window. He dropped onto a sloping porch, rolled off it, and crashed into the yard. Jessie and Ki stared down at him. For a moment, Jessie thought that the man must have broken his neck. But she was wrong. Castillo shook himself and screamed, *"Rodrigo! Amigos!"*

Jessie and Ki did not wait to hear the rest. Castillo was calling his men to come to his aid and to catch and kill the gringo invaders of his household.

"I think we had better get out of here fast," Ki said.

"What about me?" Anita cried. "He will kill me or throw me to Rodrigo and the troops!"

Ki believed her. "You're coming with us," he said leaping for the hallway. "You're the one who is going to show us the way out of here."

"But there is no way. Only through the front gate!"

Ki knew differently. "If we can reach the courtyard, we can climb the vine-covered walls and escape. But we must hurry!"

They raced down the hallway. A man came flying up the stairway and Ki met him at the top of the stairs. A brief struggle ensued; then the man grunted in pain and went crashing over backward and tumbled brokenly back down the second floor of the house. Ki, Jessie, and Anita were right behind him. They reached the ground floor and raced for the courtyard, hearing the bootheels of many running men who were pouring into the house.

"Here!" Ki said, cupping his hands for Jessie. When she placed her boot into his hands, he threw her up and she grabbed the vines and clung to the high adobe wall, then scrambled safely up to the top.

"Now you, Anita!"

She looked up at Jessie, her eyes wild with panic. "I don't think I can do it!"

"You'd better, and be quick! Hurry!"

Anita placed her sandaled foot in Ki's laced fingers. She closed her eyes and Ki heaved her upward. Jessie grabbed Anita's upraised hand before she lost her balance. For a moment, the Mexican girl hung against the wall.

"Open your damned eyes and grab a vine!" Ki shouted.

Anita obeyed. Thrashing and tearing at the wall, she lost her sandal but managed to dig her toes into the vines, tearing big hunks of foliage from the wall. But with Jessie pulling and grunting from the top, she went up and straddled the wall.

"Look out, Ki!" Jessie shouted as several of Castillo's men burst into the courtyard.

The samurai bent his legs and sprang upward, his powerful fingers reaching almost to the top of the wall. Vines broke under his weight, but he was clawing his way up as bullets from the Mexicans started to rip across the court-yard. Jessie could hear the bullets striking the wall. With one leg in the courtyard and one dangling over the outside wall, she was able to snatch her derringer back off her thigh. She fired both barrels without aiming, knowing that the stubby weapon had no accuracy.

But her shots had the desired effect. They momentarily caused Castillo's men to retreat for cover. And by the time they realized that Jessie had no more bullets, she, Ki, and the Mexican slave girl were dropping over the wall and rolling down the hillside toward the crowded streets of Juarez.

Chapter 7

Back safely in El Paso, Jessie and Ki found a place for Anita to stay, and the next morning they returned to the Texas Ranger headquarters. The old man was again sitting in Captain Jones's chair, but this day he was grim-faced and obviously upset.

Jessie pulled a chair up beside him and said, "No word yet from Captain Jones and his men?"

The old man shook his head, his lips thin and white. Jessie had a strong feeling that something had gone wrong and that he didn't want to tell her. "Listen," she said gently. "I think you've heard something that's not very good. Now, we want to help, but we can't do that if you're not willing to cooperate."

He had been staring out of the window, but now his head snapped around and he glared at her. "You and your friend were in Juarez yesterday. You went to see that son of a bitch Antonio Castillo. Don't try and deny it!"

Jessie was caught a little off guard. She glanced at Ki, whose expression revealed his own surprise. Jessie looked back at the old man. "How did you know we were at Casa Castillo?"

He almost gloated. "You think I'm as dumb as I look, don't you, lady? Well, I'm not just some old goat sitting here restin' my brains! I get paid for watchin' this office and I also get paid for listenin' to the talk on the street. And talk moves mighty fast across that big muddy river,

Miss Starbuck. Why, all of Juarez saw you, him, and Castillo's woman come racing across the border last night. What I want to know is, what the hell were you doin' over there?"

Jessie realized she had greatly underestimated this man. But now she was in a quandary: Should she tell him the entire truth and seek his help in trapping Captain Jones in his deceit, or should she be more discreet? "We came to El Paso at the request of Captain Ben Ray," she began.

"Any proof of that?" he demanded.

"Yes." Jessie turned to Ki. "Would you go to my room and get Captain Ray's letter? It's in my saddlebags."

Ki nodded and was gone. Jessie looked back to the old man. "All right," she said, "you'll have the letter in a few minutes but it only says that Captain Ray needs help and asks us to come to Austin. We did just that because Ben is an old family friend. He's almost like an uncle to me."

"Ben Ray is one of the finest men to ever pin on a badge," the old man grunted. "He and Cap'n Jones were as good a pair as ever pinned on the badge."

Jessie took a deep breath. She decided to take a gamble. If she lost, the old man might lunge for her throat; but if she won, he might break down and tell her the truth about Semus Jones and the corruption that existed in this town. "Ben asked me to help his old friend Captain Jones get out of whatever mess he's gotten himself into. There are rumors that—"

"Damn those rumors!" The old man came out of his chair in a hurry. He pointed a shaky finger at Jessie and began to yell, spittle flying from his mouth. "I know what you came here for, and you're wrong! Semus Jones ain't no traitor to his badge! Why, he'd die first!"

Jessie used a bandana to wipe her face. She realized that getting angry in return would not help matters one damn

74

bit, but this man was trying the limits of her patience. "I talked to Antonio Castillo. Even he admitted that Semus Jones was on his payroll."

"He would, that lyin' son of a bitch!"

Jessie placed her hands on her hips. "If you know something I don't that will help clear this up, then tell me, dammit! Neither I nor Ben Ray want to see your captain dragged through the mud. If Captain Jones is innocent, you'd better start talking, mister."

The old man sat down heavily. The strength and the fire washed right out of him. He clasped his bony hands together until the knuckles were white. "I can't tell you anything because even Semus won't say nothin'. But I know one damned thing and I'd stake my life on it, Miss Starbuck. If Semus is workin' with Antonio Castillo, there's a damn sight better reason for it than money. He's doin' it for somethin' else, and you can bet it's worth it. If you and your friend want the real truth about what's going on here, there's only one man who might be able to tell you."

"Who's that?"

"Giff Jones. He turned in his badge last month. Just threw it in the door and walked away without sayin' a damn word to his pa or any of the other men that he's fought side by side with for the last four or five years. Somethin' is bad wrong between old Semus and his boy. Somethin' is bad wrong about this whole damn business!"

Jessie turned to see Ki enter the Ranger headquarters with the letter that had taken her from the Circle Star roundup. "Here," she said, offering it to the old man, who sat looking miserable and bitter.

He waved her off. "I can't read noways. I guess if you brung it, it must say what you say it says. But I can tell you this: however bad it all looks, Cap'n Jones is innocent. Why, in all the years he's been a cap'n, he never once took a dollar that wasn't his own."

"But you agree that he has been working with Antonio Castillo?" Jessie said in a soft voice.

The old man nodded. "I just wish he'd have told me or Giff why."

"Maybe he did tell his son," Jessie said. "Where can I find him?"

"When he ain't bustin' men's heads or a woman's heart, Giff is a bronc-buster and a wild-horse catcher, Miss Starbuck. He and his pa have a place about fifteen miles north of town. He might be there, or he might be huntin' wild horses."

She turned to Ki. "I guess we might as well go find Giff. I met him when we were just kids. He was wild then."

"He's wilder now," the old man said. "He's a match for his father or any damned Indian or *bandito*. He can ride and rope as well as the best, and all that takes second place to his shootin'. You go out there, you'd best announce yourselves well in advance. Giff is inclined to shoot first and ask questions later."

"I thought all Texas Rangers were inclined that way," Ki said, for that certainly was their reputation.

The old man nodded. "They are, but Giff does it a little faster."

Jessie got up to leave. "I'm sorry about all this," she said, stopping at the door. "I can tell how much Captain Jones means to you, but the evidence is pretty strong against him."

The old man looked up. "I got a hunch he and the boys might be dead anyways, so it don't much matter."

Jessie started. "Why do you say that?"

"The telegraph office sent a messenger over to say that a

76

Texas Ranger's horse came gallopin' into the little town of Spur, New Mexico. I guess it musta been the cap'n's horse 'cause he always had a badge pinned to his saddle blanket. Anyways, there was blood on the saddle. You go see Giff, you tell him about it, hear me?"

Jessie nodded. "I'll tell him," she promised.

The old man sniffled. He ran his fingers over the captain's desk. "Old Semus, he's probably dead and the vultures have picked his bones clean. I feel that in my gut, Miss Starbuck. I just got a hunch Semus and the other four Rangers that went with him got themselves ambushed by the Comanche, or maybe the Apache, 'cause that's Apache country, that far west. Could be either, though, but the Apache are sneakier and Semus was a hard man to sneak up on. He still had damn good eyes and he could hear better'n most. I sure do think he's dead, Miss Starbuck."

Jessie said nothing, and the old man began to cry softly. She walked out the door with Ki following close behind her. They went to the livery and saddled their horses, and it wasn't until they were out of town and heading north to find Giff Jones that Jessie voiced her thoughts.

"If Semus Jones is dead, then I sure can't see any reason to sully his reputation or that of the Texas Rangers. Can you?"

"Nope," Ki said.

"Then we'll just bury the rumors along with his body," Jessie said. "In a way, I almost hope that's how this all works out. Be a lot better than smearing the Texas Rangers."

Ki said nothing. He had missed most of the conversation with the old man and he figured that Jessie knew more about this than he did, so he'd leave the conclusions and tough moral decisions up to her. All he cared about was seeing that they solved this riddle and then getting Jessie back safe to Circle Star. This was bad country, and if they actually followed the trail of the El Paso Texas Rangers northwest into New Mexico Territory, it was going to get worse. Maybe Giff Jones would have some easy solution. Then again, maybe he was part of the problem. Either way, things were getting more and more interesting.

Giff Jones sleeved the sweat from his eyes and smeared his face with a film of mud. The young and very inexperienced sorrel beneath him trembled with excitement and Giff had to work to keep it from bolting into the canyon just before the wild horses came surging into view. "Easy," he said. "Easy, boy."

The horse calmed a little, but then the ground began to shake and a herd of wild horses came storming down the canyon. Giff held his own mount in check just a moment longer, and when the buckskin stallion came rushing by, the Texan sank his spurs. His sorrel was still fresh, and had been chosen for its speed, stamina, and strength. Giff had his lariat up and whirling, and even though the stallion put on a sudden burst of speed, it was too slow to evade the loop that shot from Giff's big hand and sailed neatly over its head. Giff yanked on the reins and his horse squatted down in the loose rock. The buckskin was a big animal, and when it hit the end of the lariat, its momentum and power jerked Giff's sorrel right off its feet. Giff had an instant to react, and he did the only thing that he could do—kick free from his stirrups and relax his body. He felt himself being catapulted out of his saddle. When he struck the rocky ground, something in his side gave as he slammed up against a rock. He grunted, rolled, and came to a standstill, hearing his own horse screaming in pain. Giff looked up and saw that the sorrel had broken its leg in the tumble.

Worse, the buckskin stallion was picking itself up in a cloud of dust. It shook its head and rolled its eyes. Then, spotting Giff, it charged with its ears drawn back and its yellow teeth exposed. Giff staggered to his feet. His first impulse was to shoot the buckskin, but he doubted that his old Colt would stop it in its tracks. So he did what any man with any sense would do—run. He just whirled and ran for all he was worth, ignoring the cracked rib. The buckskin overhauled him and took a vicious bite out of his back. Giff hollered as the buckskin hit the end of the lariat, which was still tied to the sorrel's saddle. The shirt tore out of the stallion's teeth and Giff threw himself forward just beyond the wild horse's reach.

"Holy tamales!" he whispered, crabbing away as the buckskin reared and fought at the rope to get to him. Furious because the weight of Giff's thrashing sorrel was stopping him, the stallion whirled and went after the poor animal. Giff drew his gun and without seeming to take aim, he emptied his Colt. The unfortunate sorrel died before the stallion could stomp it to death.

Giff stood up and watched the stallion rear and strike the dead animal. "Stop it!" the Texan yelled, "or you'll bust the hell outta my saddle!"

But the buckskin didn't seem to give a damn about the saddle. It stomped the lifeless sorrel three times and then tried to run after its band of mares. It actually dragged the dead, thousand-pound saddle horse nearly fifty yards until the corpse became jammed between two big rocks.

Giff slapped the dust from his Levi's. "Now I got you, you big, ugly son of a bitch!" he whispered in a voice that was frankly admiring. "I sure didn't expect it to turn out this way, though. You cost me a good, honest young horse."

Giff hobbled forward. He moved into the rocks, and it

took him only a few minutes to reach his dead horse and snatch a second lariat from his battered saddle. He formed a loop and his second toss went straight for the stallion's hind legs. The horse felt the rope, and it kicked instinctively. Giff used that reaction to yank tight the noose around the stallion's rear legs. Taking a half-hitch around his hips, Giff used his power and leverage to throw the buckskin off balance and then crashing to the earth. Quick as his broken rib would allow, and keeping a constant tension on the leg-rope, he transferred it from his hips to a scrubby oak tree, and then tied it fast.

The stallion was down, nearly helpless. Caught between the weight of Giff's dead horse and the strength of the tree, it fought hard, but it tired after thirty minutes or so and lay with its sides heaving and breath tearing in and out of its distended nostrils.

Giff leisurely finished his Mexican cigarillo and studied the buckskin. "I'm holding you responsible for the loss of my own horse. A damn good horse, if he'd have lived long enough to get more experience carrying a rider. So you're going to have to take his place, mister. But the first thing we're going to do is to castrate you so you'll be a little more mannerly."

Giff moved toward the stallion. As he did, he removed his bandana. He seemed to be in no hurry to do anything, but when the buckskin's head snaked for his leg, Giff jumped on it. He slapped the bandana across the horse's eyes and tied it tight. Blinded, the animal thrashed wildly, and when it tired even more Giff removed a set of small hobbles from his saddlebags. He got them on the buckskin's rear hocks, then used the second rope to hog-tie the stallion.

Taking his knife from his pocket, he exposed the blade and bent over the stallion. He hefted the animal's ponderous testicles and said, "This almost hurts me as much as it'll hurt you."

The stallion thrashed helplessly and Giff, as always, felt a twinge of guilt and hesitated. He did not like to do this; it sort of made his own gonads suck up a little. But it was necessary. Besides, he rationalized, a stallion had three, maybe four years of real breeding time, and then it would be killed or crippled by a younger one of its kind and run off to eventually fall prey to wolves. But a good saddle horse might have ten years or more of work in him, and Giff treated his horses with kindness.

The blade of the knife was razor-sharp but the stallion still went crazy as its sack was rudely violated and the thick white cords were sliced away. Giff removed the bloody testicles and hurled them into the rocks. The gelding groaned and lay still. Giff moved up to its head and stroked the blinded beast. "I am sorry," he confessed. "You and me are gonna be friends after a few days. You're the horse I've been wanting for almost two years now. We'll ride a lot of good trails together. And that's a promise."

The buckskin was covered with sweat and it was trembling as if chilled to the bone. But Giff kept stroking its coat. By sunset, it was quiet and the bleeding had stopped. Giff treated himself to another cigarillo and watched the sun go down. Mustanging wasn't as exciting as being a Texas Ranger on patrol, but it came mighty close.

★

Chapter 8

"It isn't exactly Circle Star," Ki said drily, as they dismounted in front of Giff Jones's horse ranch.

Jessie studied the corrals, which were made of heavy logs: the only solid looking thing on the place. She knew enough about horses to see that Giff had built his breaking corral and horse pens with a great deal of effort. There were a few gates and runways that showed that the man knew what he was doing when it came to handling wild horses.

"There's no one here," Ki said.

Jessie nodded. She rode Sun over to the water trough and let the animal drink its fill. A tumbleweed bounced across the small ranchyard and came to a stop against a rickety fence. The house, if you wanted to flatter it by using the term, was small: little more than a two- or three-room cabin. There were no windows, only rifle ports. Jessie could see that the door was padlocked. She studied the signs around the place but there were few to tell her how long the man had been gone.

"Shall we go hunting, or wait?" Ki asked, watering his own horse before they each dismounted and drank.

"Why don't you see if you can pick up his tracks in the mesquite. If we can do that, we might as well go after him. He could be gone for days."

"Maybe even weeks," the samurai said, handing her the reins and moving to the perimeter of the ranchyard. Jessie studied the house. A woman might once have lived in that place, but that was a long time ago and there were few signs of her passing. Just a little border of rock ran along the front of the house. Most of it was gone, but enough remained to suggest an abandoned flower garden. There had once been front windows, two of them. But they had long ago been boarded over and there were more than a dozen bullet holes in their coverings.

Jessie had always believed that you could tell a lot about a person by his home, but she could not get much of a feel for the Joneses except that they were no-nonsense, and that they sure weren't spending any of Castillo's payoff money on this poor horse ranch. There wasn't much here to look at. Just the house, the fine corrals, a lean-to shed, a small barn, and the well and the water trough. That was it: the sum of a man's accumulations after being a Texas Ranger for most of his life. The saying was that no Ranger ever pinned on his badge for the money, and if this was the best that a full captain, a living legend, could do for himself, then things were grim indeed. Why, Jessie had seen better homesteads among men who worked in fields and laundries. It just seemed to her that a man who had risked his life for Texas so many years ought to be better compensated.

"Maybe they're drinkers or gamblers," she said aloud to herself. "Maybe they spend all their money on women or mescal." She checked her cinch, found it loose, and tightened it. "Whatever, they sure don't spend it here."

Ki seemed to be thinking the same things. "I'd have thought they'd do better," he said. "They must be putting all of Antonio Castillo's money in a bank somewhere."

"Yes," Jessie said, "they must be."

"I found his tracks. They're only about two days old."

Jessie reined her horse around. "Then let's go find him."

Ki nodded. He wondered if Jessie was going to state flat-out that she knew that Semus was in cahoots with Castillo. If she did, Ki knew that he had better be prepared to defend her. This Giff Jones had the reputation of being a fighter, a man fast with his fists or a gun. The samurai rode along beside Jessie. He liked the way that she went straight at things. Maybe sometimes she did get in over her head and needed a little help, but she was more often on firm footing. Like down in Juarez. By the time he and Anita had reached Castillo's bedroom, Jessie had already found out what she wanted to know. She'd drawn her derringer and had everything under control. Ki still grinned when he remembered the expression on Castillo's face.

They rode steadily all the rest of the day and started early the next morning. It was almost noon when Ki said, "What is that sound?"

Jessie turned her head from the wind. Now she heard the sound. "It's a horse squealing and running. No, not running, bucking."

"I think we've found our man," Ki said, pointing to a big cloud of dust that just now came billowing over a low hill ahead of them.

Jessie nodded and spurred Sun into a gallop. When she topped the hill and looked down at the man and the bucking horse, she knew at once that this was ex-Ranger Giff Jones. Jessie remembered she had once been quite smitten with Giff. Even as a boy, he had been tall, wide-shouldered and very handsome. But he had been several years older than her, and he'd paid her no mind. Now, as she viewed him through a dust-cloud, she could see that he had turned into a fine specimen of manhood. And what a ride he was making!

Jessie reined her own horse to a standstill and sat watching with open admiration. Giff was atop a powerful buckskin, and he was riding the bucking, plunging animal as if he were nailed to the saddle. There was no anger or cruelty in his method, either; a fact that she very much appreciated. He was spurring, yes, quirting, yes—but in neither case was there evidence of anger or unnecessary force being used.

The buckskin was sunfishing and was obviously a hard bucker. It went right up in the air and then seemed to snap in the middle so that its head and its hind end almost came together. Like a spring, it snapped back straight. When it landed, it did so on all fours. A pile-driving bronc like that would snap a man's neck, and it was easy to see that every time Giff took the impact of the landing, his head would whip. He seemed to be having some pain in his left side and Jessie guessed that he had an injured rib.

But despite the fact that this sagebrush bronc-buster was taking a heavy pounding, it was clear that he was in control of the buckskin and content to let it buck itself out rather than drive it into a run. The horse had its head down and every time it hit the ground it grunted loudly. To Jessie, there was something terrible and at the same time beautiful about a man and a bronc engaged in that first great struggle, each out to destroy the other. And though some might insist that the man had all the advantages, that was not necessarily true. More than one of her own bronc-busters had been pitched so hard he'd never wanted to ride wild horses again. The buckskin was strong and determined, but, as the animal's strength waned in the struggle, it became apparent that it was simply no match for the sinewy horseman who clung to its back.

The fight ended with a few crow-hops. Then the buck-skin began to trot, every movement an effort. It was covered with lather and dripping wet, and Giff Jones neither pushed it nor pulled it to a stop. He simply let the horse jog along until it decided on its own to stop and wait to see what would happen next.

Giff saw them and he plow-reined the weary buckskin in their general direction. The horse stumbled with fatigue and Giff gave it a nudge with his spurs. The buckskin responded with a token bucking motion that made the man smile. He drew the horse up to Jessie and Ki and studied them for several moments before he spoke. "Well I'll be," he said. "There aren't any other beautiful women who ride stirrup to stirrup alongside a samurai. So young Jessica Starbuck has come to pay me a visit. I must be dreaming."

Had the circumstances which brought her to this man been more pleasant, Jessie would have laughed. But seeing as they were not, she had to force a smile. She said, "That was quite a display of bronc riding, Giff. It's been a while since I've seen better."

He thumbed his Stetson back on his head. "I doubt you've ever seen better, Jessie. Not even those *vaqueros* you hire can put on a better show that I can."

"Are you always so modest?"

He chuckled. "I shoot and fight even better than I ride. What brings you to this country? You come to find Semus?"

"Yes," she told him.

"Why?" His smile faded. He had dark blue eyes, and sandy colored hair that was long enough to touch his broad shoulders. He wore a mustache and a three-day growth of beard. He was dirty and she could smell his rank maleness from six feet away.

"I think you know why," she said in a quiet voice as she waited to judge his reaction. It would tell her plenty.

He exploded in anger. "If I knew why, I damn sure wouldn't have asked!"

Ki rode his horse in between them. "Don't shout at the lady," he said in a reasonable tone of voice that was firm, but certainly not threatening.

Giff dug his spurs into the buckskin's side and the big horse jumped right at Ki. It struck Ki's smaller mount with its powerful shoulder and then bit the horse at the same moment that Giff's fist crashed against the side of the samurai's head, unhorsing him to the ground.

Jessie threw herself off Sun and was at Ki's side in an instant. She looked up to see Giff riding the buckskin away at a gallop. "Are you all right?" she asked the samurai.

Ki nodded. His head was ringing and the entire side of his face was numb. "I've never been hit any harder than that," he said, opening and closing his jaw to make sure that it wasn't broken. The samurai caught his horse up and swung into his saddle. "Wait here, please," he said.

"But—" Jessie didn't want to wait.

The samurai raised his hand. "I ask you this as a favor."

"But why? I'm not squeamish and maybe I can help..."

"Help me?" The samurai grinned like a boy with candy. "I will try not to hurt him too badly, Jessie. But such bad manners deserve a stern lesson."

"He may prove to be more difficult than you expect," Jessie said. "He was supposed to be the toughest of the Texas Rangers."

Ki turned his horse and sent it after the big man on the buckskin. He knew that Jessie's warning was worth heeding. This man might be his equal. If he pulled that big Colt on his hip, Ki knew that he was going to be in serious difficulty, for he had left his bow and arrows in his El Paso hotel room.

Ki was not nearly the horseman that Giff Jones had already proven himself to be, but the buckskin was still weak from its castration and its fight with Giff and easily overtaken. As soon as he realized that he was being followed, Giff turned his horse around and waited.

"You want some more, or what?" he asked.

Ki dismounted. "I think I would."

Giff took a deep breath and dismounted. He took his lariat and tied the buckskin's hoof up close to the cinch so that it could not run away. "Then let's settle this right now," he said, doubling up his big fists and marching forward.

Ki waited. He stood easy, but very light on his feet. When the powerful man cocked his right fist and let it fly, the samurai ducked and slammed his elbow into Giff's busted ribcage. The man groaned in pain, staggered, but somehow kept his feet. He was as strong as the horses he broke. He grabbed Ki and hurled him to the ground. Ki rolled as Giff came down with his knees. Before the man could rise, Ki's foot came up and caught Giff under the jaw. The man crashed over backward and came up scratching and fighting mad.

"All right, so we kick a little!" Giff shouted, lashing out with his boot. His legs were very long but he was off balance, and Ki was able to cut his standing leg out from under him and bring him to the ground. Ki chopped down with the edge of his hand and caught his opponent just beneath the jaw. Giff choked, and struggled to get to his feet.

Ki backed off. The big ex-Ranger came forward more cautiously. He feinted a right. When Ki jumped back, he sprang forward and caught the samurai up in his powerful arms. Ki managed to trip him and they toppled to the ground and rolled. Giff outweighed Ki by fifty pounds, and he was easily the stronger. He drove his head into Ki's face and then tried to crush him in his arms. The samurai struggled. He felt as if his chest was about to collapse. Somehow he managed to get one arm free, and he reached up and drove his thumb into an *atemi* point at the base of Giff's thick neck. But it wasn't easy. Giff was so muscular that cutting off the blood supply to his brain and rendering him unconscious was a formidable task, one made all the more difficult by Giff, who kept slamming the top of his head into Ki's face. But at last Ki felt the man go limp in his arms.

The samurai broke free from the man's crushing embrace. He sucked air into his constricted lungs. On his hands and knees, he let his head hang down while blood seeped from his battered face. After several moments, he climbed unsteadily to his feet. If ever he had to fight Giff Jones again, he would immediately use a sweep lotus to the throat or a snap-kick to the groin. That was the only way to stop this horse of a man before he inflicted very serious damage.

Ki looked up and saw Jessie come riding over and dismount. "I have a confession to make," she said, putting her arm around Ki's shoulders and staring down at the unconscious man. "I watched. You really had your hands full this time. Why didn't you use a sweep lotus or snap-kick?"

"Because," Ki said, "I admired his fighting ability too much to have it end with a single blow. I wanted to see how good he was."

"And?"

Ki shrugged. "It is a good thing that my old friend Hirata taught me *atemi*. Otherwise, it would have been very bad for me indeed."

Jessie could not have agreed more. Giff Jones had given the samurai quite a pounding. "How long will he be out?" she asked.

"A long time," Ki replied. "I did not have time to use refinement."

Jessie frowned. "I think we had better tie him across my saddle."

"And what will you ride?"

Jessie motioned toward the buckskin. "I can see by the dried blood on the inside of his legs that he won't be back to normal for a few more days. Besides, he's just been busted."

Ki did not like the idea of Jessie riding that wild horse. But she was a fine horsewoman, a far better rider than himself. "He looked pretty 'normal' to me when this man was breaking him a few minutes ago."

"I'll be fine," Jessie said, dodging the buckskin's flashing teeth as it tried to bite her. Jessie vaulted lightly into the saddle. She reached down, and, with a tug on the rope, untied the leg. The buckskin, once more on all four feet and having caught its breath, decided that it might be able to shed itself of this new, much lighter rider. It tried to get its head down between its legs but Jessie wouldn't quite allow that to happen.

The buckskin took the best that it could get. It snapped up into the air and sunfished. Jessie's hat went sailing and she rammed her spurs into the horse's tender ribs. The buckskin grunted with pain. The fight went out of it, though it did buck a few more times out of pride.

Ki managed to get the tall bronc-buster across Jessie's saddle. He tied the man hand and foot under Sun's belly and then he also mounted.

"I noticed that you tied him good and tight and took his gun," she told the samurai.

"I'm no fool," Ki said. "Given the chance, when he wakes up and discovers where he is, his first instinct will be to kill me."

Jessie studied the unconscious man. "I think you're right. And I guess the safest thing we could do would be to take him right on into El Paso and jail him at Ranger headquarters until he decides to cooperate."

"If we ride all day and all night, we could be there by dawn."

"Can you keep him out that long?"

The samurai nodded.

"Then that's what we'll do," she said. "Giff reminds me of a mountain lion. He needs to be put in a cage until he settles down and acts human."

Ki agreed. His nose was throbbing and his face was battered worse than it had been in a long, long time. He wasn't afraid of Giff Jones, but neither was he eager to tangle with the man again. Given those truths, he was plenty willing to ride all night.

Chapter 9

When they hauled Giff Jones into the Ranger headquarters, the old man almost went beserk.

"Are you crazy?" he screamed. "When Giff wakes up, he'll tear this place apart!"

Ki tested every bar in the cell. "I don't think so," he said, satisfied that the Ranger jail was plenty strong enough to hold any man. "But I'm sure he'll try."

"What charges have you arrested him on?"

Jessie gave that one a few seconds of thought. "For his own safe-keeping," she said at last. "You see, he has this self-destructive tendency to attack my friend Ki. We don't want that to happen again."

The old man wasn't buying it. "Your friend's face looks a hell of a lot worse than Giff's."

"Maybe so," Jessie replied, "but we're going to keep him locked up until he decides he wants to be reasonable. And if that doesn't sit right with you, then I'm afraid that we'll have to toss you out."

Now the old man really had a fit. "Try it!" he raged. "I was given the authority to be here by Cap'n Jones hisself and I'll fight to the death before either of you toss me out!"

Jessie frowned. "Then will you give me your word you won't try and release Giff the moment that we turn our backs?"

"I'll do no such thing!"

"Jessie," Ki said. "He's left us no choice."

"I'm afraid you're right."

"Wait a derned minute! What are you two fixin' to do with me?"

"Better lock him up," Jessie said to the samurai.

The old man threw himself at Ki but the samurai whacked him once across the side of the head. Then, while he was still dazed, he tossed him into the cell with Giff. Ki went in and made sure that the man didn't have a spare set of cell keys in his pocket; then he locked the door.

"That ought to hold them until we get ourselves some breakfast," Jessie said wearily.

Ki was famished. They had not eaten since early yesterday and he felt the need for some nourishment. "Let's go," he said, taking Jessie's arm. "When those two wake up, there's going to be hell to pay in that cell."

Jessie looked at the powerful young Giff Jones and then at the old man. "I would say you're right."

They had a good big breakfast, and they did not hurry themselves over coffee. But when they returned, both Giff and the old man were shouting at the tops of their voices for help. They were both nearly insane with fury, and it was fortunate that the Ranger headquarters was made out of thick adobe; otherwise they'd have brought half of El Paso on the run.

"I think you'd both better settle down and get reasonable," Jessie said, as she surveyed the unlikely pair.

"The only thing that will make a reasonable man out of me," Giff shouted, "is for you to let me the hell out of this cell so I can throttle your samurai and then put you over my knee and whomp your shapely behind!"

Jessie shrugged. "In that case, you're in for a long stay. That's mighty unfortunate, considering your father's saddle."

Giff blinked. "What are you talking about?"

"Why don't you tell him," she said to the old man.

"What the deuce is she talking about, Art!"

In the face of Giff's wrath, the old man shrank back against the bars of the cell. "Well," he wheedled, "it's just that the cap'n's horse showed up near Spur, New Mexico."

Giff reached out, took a fistful of Art's shirtfront and balled it up as he drew the old man to him. "My pa would never let his horse run away and leave him on foot in Apache country. What else is there you haven't told me?"

"Breaking his neck isn't going to help your father," Jessie said. "The facts are that your father's horse was found galloping into Spur with blood on the saddle."

Giff released the old man. "How much blood?" he said in a voice barely above a whisper.

"I don't think they said in the telegraph, did they?" Jessie said.

Art shook his head. "He's probably still alive, Giff. You know he's too damn tough and ornery to kill."

Giff gripped the bars in his big hands and pressed his forehead against them. "What about the others?" he asked. "He rode out with some damned good men. What about them?"

"No news," Jessie said, seeing how shaken the man was.

"Miss Starbuck, let me out of here," Giff demanded. "I'm heading for Spur."

Jessie folded her arms over her chest. "Not without us, and we're not leaving without some rest for ourselves and our horses."

"What business is this of yours?" Giff demanded. "You're not Texas Rangers."

"According to Art," Jessie said pointedly, "neither are you."

"That's right, but he's my father."

"And he's Captain Ben Ray's friend. Ben asked Ki and me to come help your father any way we could. It seems that we could be useful in New Mexico."

Giff swore. "So," he said raggedly, "even old Ben is starting to believe all the ugly rumors about my father and Antonio Castillo."

Jessie clamped her mouth shut. She saw absolutely no point in telling Giff that she had learned from Castillo's own mouth, that the allegations against Captain Jones were based on fact and much more than just malicious gossip.

"We can talk about what we've heard or not heard later," Ki said, understanding Jessie's silence and approving.

The young man behind the cell bars looked angry enough to explode, and it took all of his willpower to control himself enough to say, "You've got until tonight. I'll wait that long."

Ki stepped forward. "You'll wait until we let you out of the cell. Jessie, just to make sure that he keeps his word, I suggest you leave him and Art locked up until this evening."

Jessie fully agreed. "I'll have some food sent over," she told the two men, who stared at her with disbelief.

"Now wait just a damn minute!" Giff bellowed, shaking the bars. "You can't do this to us!"

"That's right!" Art raged. "Why. . ."

Jessie and Ki did not wait to hear any more. They would sleep until early evening. Then they would release Giff, and together they would ride northwest. Maybe Captain Jones was still alive, but somehow Jessie doubted it, and she suspected that Giff did too. A Texas Ranger taught his horse to ground-tie, and if he was going to be gone any length of time, he either tied the animal securely to a tree or else he hobbled the horse to ensure that it did not run away. It didn't take much deduction to see that blood on the saddle of a riderless horse meant some kind of bad trouble.

Jessie felt alive again after a bath, eight hours of sleep, and a good dinner as she and Ki returned to release Giff and Art from the Ranger cell.

"I ought to tear you apart," Giff said to Ki as the cell was opened.

"You tried it once and failed; you'd do no better a second time. Probably much worse."

Giff pushed out of the cell and the old man followed. "We'll need rifles and plenty of ammunition in addition to our Colt revolvers," he said, marching over to the rifle rack and selecting several Winchesters. "Were the horses grained and fed while I was locked up?"

Now that he was out of the cell, Jessie could not help feel a little intimidated by his anger. She squared her shoulders. "The horses are ready and so are we."

He finished loading the rifles. "If you have your rifles, say so; otherwise we take these."

"I have my own," Jessie said.

"What about you, samurai?"

Ki turned. "I have a bow and arrows. Other weapons as well. I don't need a rifle."

"The hell you say!" Giff growled. "The Apache and the Comanche are both the finest bowmen in America."

Ki said nothing, but he did not reach out for a rifle.

"I'll bring an extra along," Giff said with a trace of disgust, "just in case you snap your bowstring."

Ki ignored the cutting remark. Insults did not bother him very much, except those about his ancestry. Being called a "Chink" or even a Chinaman was about the only insult that really rankled him. And because of the Chinese influx into California during the Forty-niner gold rush and

97

twenty years later when they were imported to build the famous transcontinental railroad, almost every Oriental on the American frontier was assumed to be a Chinaman. Why couldn't whites realize that the Chinese and the Japanese hated each other? The two nationalities had never been on good terms. To Ki, they didn't even look the same.

"Let's go," Giff said brusquely. "Spur is one hell of a long ways off across bad country. If we don't run into Indians, then we'll likely run into either the Comancheros or Mexican bandits."

"And if we do, will you want to fight them, or just try and avoid trouble until you reach Spur and find out about your father?"

Giff hesitated, filling the doorway. "Avoid trouble? Miss Starbuck, I don't know how to avoid trouble, and neither does my father. We just make a habit of going through trouble. Does that answer your question?"

"Yes," Jessie said. "I just thought it was important to know where you stand."

"Well, now you know," he said, moving to the hitching rail. "And I can tell you and Ki something else as well. You either keep up with me or I leave you. I won't coddle you just because you happen to be rich and pretty."

Jessie almost laughed out loud, which was better than getting angry. "In the first place, Ki and I are as well mounted as you and considerably lighter. Our horses will match that buckskin bronc you're taking. And in the second place, we've ridden halfway across Texas in the hope of clearing your father's name. We're not about to be stopped now. Have I made that very plain?"

Giff nodded. He checked his cinch and then mounted the buckskin. The horse bucked a little but not with any real spirit. Giff pulled his Stetson down low over his eyes.

"Both this horse and I have seen happier days, Miss Star-buck, but I guess we'll take you and Ki on a ride you'll never forget."

"Why don't you call me Jessie?"

He actually smiled. "Why, Jessie, I believe I will. Let's ride! Guard the fort, Art!"

The old man nodded. He looked stooped and very old, and Jessie knew that he had been humbled by his detention in the jail cell. She hoped that his spirits would recover by the time they got back—if they got back.

Chapter 10

They had followed the Rio Grande as it wound its way north between the Mimbres and the San Andres mountain ranges. Las Cruces was a blistering, sun-drenched mining camp where men fought for gold as well as survival against raiding Indians, and the threesome spent only a few hours there getting supplies. Spur was even farther north, an embattled mining camp constantly under siege by the Indians.

Day after day Jessie and Ki followed the tall Texas Ranger. He started early in the morning, halted at noon and napped for several hours during the hottest part of the day, then arose to ride until nearly midnight, when they made a cold camp beneath a glittering shower of stars.

"You are a very quiet man," Jessie said late one night as they neared Spur and made camp. "Have you always been this way?"

He looked at her. "Pretty much. My pa is quiet until aroused to passion. He always said that actions spoke louder than words. He said that there were already enough words captured on the pages of books, newspapers, and gazettes to fill the world with noise. No sense in adding extra, is there?"

Jessie thought that was a curious way to put things. "Tell me about your father. I've heard the stories. I know he's a legend in Texas, and Ben said they had fought together down in Mexico City."

"They fought a hell of a lot of other places too," Giff

101

said, shifting his back against the underside of his saddle and preparing to sleep. "I guess that's what hurts me most of all."

Jessie peered at him in the moonlight. She could not read his expression. "What do you mean by that?"

"I mean that a man who has been a friend of my pa's as long as Captain Ray ought to be ashamed of himself for even considering that Pa would throw in with the likes of Antonio Castillo."

Jessie glanced at Ki. She did not wish to start a confrontation here and now, but she felt strongly that she had to defend Captain Ben Ray. "Your father has been seen many times in Juarez with Castillo."

Ki tensed, ready to strike if Giff lost his temper.

"Aren't you going to say anything?" Jessie asked.

"What's there to say?" Giff shifted his weight. "You tell me a lot of folks have seen Pa with Castillo; what kind of answer can I give to that?"

"The truth. Has your father dealt with Castillo?"

Giff studied her intently. "Jessie," he said finally, "some things in life ain't always what they appear to be on first glance."

"I know," she said in reply, "but if a man is innocent of charges, he has to defend himself and his reputation."

"I thought men were innocent until proven guilty."

"Not on the Texas frontier," Jessie said. "And not when it involves a famous captain of the Texas Rangers and a known Mexican outlaw who obviously commands enormous power on the border."

Jessie tried a different tack. "I imagine you're wondering what I did when I went to see Señor Castillo."

Giff shrugged his wide shoulders. "I've been thinking about it, sure. But I reckon that was between you and him."

Jessie had to struggle to curb her anger. "I pretended to be a rich widow looking for cheap cattle. Stolen cattle. I offered to buy them from Castillo if he could guarantee that your father, Captain Jones, would not arrest me and confiscate the herd as soon as it crossed the Rio Grande."

"And I'll bet he agreed to that, didn't he?" Giff said.

Jessie was thrown off balance. "Why . . . yes he did."

Giff's voice took on a hard edge. "What else did you expect him to say in order to make the sale? He'd have promised you every longhorn he delivered would drop golden eggs if that was what you wanted to hear."

"Then it's not true, about your father?"

Giff leaned back and pulled his Stetson over his face. "Get some sleep and stop asking so damned many fool questions," he growled.

In a very few minutes, Giff was snoring softly but Jessie could not sleep at all. She kept going over and over their brief conversation, seeking some fault in his words, some inflection in his voice that would tell her what he really believed. It was a wasted mental effort. She gave it up after a few hours and forced her mind to go blank and then she slept.

"Wake up!" Ki said, nudging her softly. "He's gone."

Jessie woke up in a hurry. The sun was just coming off the horizon, and it was cool, without a cloud in the sky. She struggled to pull her boots on. "Where could he have gone?"

Ki expelled a deep breath and said, "About three thours ago I woke up hearing something that didn't fit in this country. I thought about Indians and walked about five miles to that distant butte over there."

He pointed and Jessie saw the butte. "Did you see any Indians?"

"Yes. It was still dark but I could hear the hooves of their unshod horses. They were coming directly toward our camp. I started back on the run. When I got here, Giff was already gone. He'd used himself as a decoy. The Indians crossed his trail about two miles ahead and went after him. I also found this scribbled note."

Jessie took it and read just five words: SEE YOU IN SPUR, MAYBE.

She sat up and knuckled the sleep from her eyes. "Could you tell how many Indians there were?"

"At least twenty. When the light gets stronger, I can tell better by studying their tracks."

Jessie shook her head. "Twenty or thirty, what does it matter? We have to go after him, Ki. We can't just let those Indians ride him down somewhere out in this godforsaken country."

"I know." The samurai shook his head. "But it may already be too late."

"Why do you say that?" Jessie asked with alarm.

"His horse," Ki said. "I noticed last night just before we stopped to make this camp that the buckskin was favoring its right foreleg."

Jessie groaned. "And neither you nor him said anything?"

"I thought that the animal might be stronger this morning. And maybe Giff did too."

Jessie stood up and grabbed her saddle and bridle. "Semus Jones and Spur will have to wait a little longer."

"It's not what he wanted," Ki said. "You could see by the note that he wanted us to go on to Spur."

"The hell with what he wanted!" Jessie said hotly. "He risked his own life to save ours. I'll be damned if I'll let him get away with that and not pay him the favor back."

Ki nodded and grabbed his own saddle. When Jessie

spoke in that tone of voice, he knew that the die was cast. There would be no changing her mind until they either saved Giff or determined that he had eluded the Indians and gotten away safe.

"What do you think they are?" Jessie asked as she hurriedly mounted her tall palomino. "Apache or Comanche?"

"Apache."

Jessie shook her head hopelessly. "I was afraid that you were going to say that. I was hoping it would be Comanche. We might have a better chance with them in this kind of rugged country."

Ki nodded. It was true. The Comanche were better fighters on horseback than on foot. This kind of terrain was too rough for the type of fighting they preferred. It was better suited to the Apache, who were more inclined to rely on stealth and deception to gain advantage before they struck. Ki had decided not to tell Jessie that the buckskin was favoring its right front hoof. The indentation was softer, and that meant that the horse wasn't putting the full share of his weight on that foot.

No one had to explain to the samurai that a white man mounted on a lame horse being chased by a horde of Apache stood almost no chance of survival. The odds were that Giff would be dead by midmorning.

Giff was headed back for the Rio Grande, which lay only about seven miles from last night's camp. He figured the buckskin just might last that long, and if he could get to the river and ride the animal up the current, he might be able to elude the Apache for a while—long enough for Jessie and Ki to get on into Spur, where they would be protected against attack.

But the buckskin gelding was laboring and felt as if its front end was going to crumble any minute. Giff cussed with frustration. If they'd just have pushed on for another hour or so last night, they'd have reached Spur and been safe. It was a small mining settlement and certainly easily penetrated by the Indians, but the last time that Giff had ridden through, there had been at least twenty heavily armed miners willing and able to defend themselves.

"Come on, Buck," Giff urged the faltering buckskin. "Can't you smell that lazy river just up ahead? We get there, you drink well, and I'll turn you free again. You can either run for it, or take your chances with the Indians. Either way, it'll be out of my hands. But if I was you, I'd run for it, Buck. I think we've got Apache hot on our trail and there's nothing except a man's liver roasted over the coals that they like to eat any better than horsemeat."

Almost as if the buckskin understood, it made a last, desperate effort to reach the river, and when it flew over the bank and landed in the muddy water it discovered that the river was deep, and it began to swim. The buckskin swam for all it was worth, and Giff let it go with the current instead of against it as he had originally intended. He now reasoned that the Apache would naturally assume he would try to reach the safety of Spur. In fact, on the lame horse that was an impossibility. Maybe at least by turning downriver and letting the buckskin swim with the current he would gain some precious time over the Apache. There was another advantage to heading away from Spur, and that was to allow Jessie and Ki an unobstructed run for that tiny mining community.

They were sailing along fine, and when Giff looked back over his shoulders with his two Winchesters held high and dry, he could not see any Indians on the horizon. He and the buckskin were sweeping around a sharp bend in the river when suddenly, just ahead, Giff saw a huge cotton-wood tree. It had massive roots sticking out of the water, and he guessed that about a third of its great branches were also sticking above the surface of the Rio Grande. But it was the roots and branches lurking below the water that worried Giff. As they swept in toward the tree, he tried desperately to rein his swimming mount toward the west bank of the river. But the buckskin was too played out. It had expended the last of its reserves and there was simply no more to give.

"I'm damned sorry about this," Giff said bitterly as the water swept them into the sharp roots and branches. "Damn sorry."

He winced with pain as a branch as big around as his leg lanced into the floundering buckskin. He felt the poor animal shudder as the current impaled the branch deeper into its body. Giff could not leave the animal to suffer while he swam for his life. He drew his sixgun, pressed it to the back of the buckskin's head, and pulled the trigger. The animal died in an instant, but Giff knew his act of mercy had cost him precious minutes while the Apache might have galloped upriver.

"The hell with it!" he raged, quite sure that they would kill him anyway. He untied his saddlebags, and, with two rifles in his arms, he leaped into the half submerged cottonwood tree and struggled to keep from slipping on its mossy surface as he made his way unsteadily toward the west bank. When he came to the splayed roots, he prayed that the river was shallow enough so that he could keep his rifles and ammunition dry. Giff took one look back at the dead horse and his good bronc-busting saddle; then he jumped.

The water was only chest high, but the current was strong. He stumbled over a hidden branch and almost toppled face first into the current. Somehow, he kept both rifles and his saddlebags dry. He slogged out of the water and up to the muddy west bank. The Apache had seen him and were coming on the run. Giff yanked open the cover of his saddlebags and spread the rifle cartridges out in a nice, neat line. Satisfied that he had done all that could be done in preparation, he waded out to the tree again and laid one rifle across the cradling arms of some of the roots where he could snatch it and begin firing instantly. He rested the other rifle across a thick limb and then he levered a shell into the chamber and took aim on the lead Apache.

The rifle bucked against his shoulder and it felt solid and good. The explosion and smoke blanketed the Rio Grande and seemed to sweep over the charging Indians, who had just entered the water. His first bullet scored dead center, and then he began to shoot as fast as he could lever the rifle. He poured such a deadly volley into the Indians that they broke their charge even before their horses began to swim. In utter confusion, shouting and waving their own rifles, lances, bows and arrows, they retreated back to the east bank and didn't stop running until they were out of Giff's rifle range.

They had paid dearly. The bodies of three Apache floated face down as the current carried them away. Two more were dead on the far shore, and a third was wounded and trying to crawl away. Giff let him go. He took no pleasure in killing. He shot to kill only when it really counted.

Feeling quite pleased with himself for the moment, Giff waded back to the west bank, where he calmly reloaded the empty rifle. The Apache would not try to charge him across the river in broad daylight again. That had proven to be a near suicidal course of action, and no matter what anybody said, the Apache warrior was no more eager to die than a white man. He would not hesitate to give his life in battle, but never foolishly.

Giff peered up at the sun. The Apache would cross the Rio Grande both above and below him and then gallop up the west bank and catch him in a crossfire. Of course, then he would have no place to run and no place to hide. If it were later, much later, darkness might have given him the cover to escape. But it was still very early and there would be no escape. Only death.

"They'll pay dearly," he said. "And they will damn sure not take me alive."

Chapter 11

Giff watched the Apache separate into two groups. They rode north and south along the west bank of the river until they were well out of his range. Each group then swam the river, thereby placing themselves in position to pincer him in a deadly crossfire. Had it been dark, he would have tried to swim underwater and hope that, by some miracle, he could pass by them in the swift current. Or, if he'd still had the buckskin and it were sound, he'd have hopped into the saddle and tried to swim back across the river and up the other side. With luck, Jessie and Ki would already be in Spur and he might make it there before they overtook him from behind. But the buckskin was dead and his luck had run cold.

Giff saluted the Apache and said, "If you're bound and determined to go through with this business, then I guess it's a big die-up time for all of us." Giff waded out and rested his rifle across the moss-covered tree. He took aim on the Apache to the north. He would kill as many as possible and then swing around and empty the first Winchester at the ones coming up from the south. Then, if he were still alive and they weren't driving their lances into his body, he'd grab the second Winchester and shoot until they killed him or he killed every last one.

The Apache seemed to steel themselves for the attack; then they howled and came charging in from both sides. An inexperienced Indian fighter would have panicked and

111

tried to shoot both vanguards but Giff turned his back on one group and concentrated his fire on the other. His aim was devastating, and as he worked the lever of his rifle and fired, riderless Apache ponies began to materialize through the smoke. Suddenly, with only four riders left, the group broke apart and wheeled off in retreat.

But the other body of Apache was closing in fast. Giff swung around and fired two more rounds until his rifle was empty. He dropped it in the river and snatched the second rifle from its resting place in the tree. He shot two Apache without even seeming to aim. But as he tried to bring his rifle to bear on a third, a bullet slammed into his shoulder and spun him completely around in the fast river. His rifle expended a harmless bullet into the churning water and Giff struggled to bring it back up level. An Apache warrior with a bow and arrow was charging across the riverbank, sending sheets of water high into the air. Giff managed to get his rifle braced against his shoulder and take aim. He fired just as the warrior released his arrow. Giff saw the Apache flip completely over the back of his running horse. With the others almost on top of him, Giff did the only thing he could do to save his life: he dove under the water.

He was a strong swimmer, but a bullet in the shoulder put him at a serious disadvantage. The current sent him spinning around in circles. Giff struck an underwater rock with his wounded shoulder. He grunted with pain and clawed toward the surface, knowing that he could not hold his breath a second longer. When his head cleared, he was about ten yards below the Apache. They were looking for him. A warrior raised his lance to spear Giff like a big catfish, and there was nothing the ex–Texas Ranger could do but try to get back under water. He dove, but the lance cut wickedly into his cartridge belt and then buried itself into his holster. Giff twisted and managed to get his hands on the lance. He spun around in the current, and when he surfaced, he found himself almost directly underneath an Apache pony. Its rider jumped for Giff and died on the lance.

Suddenly, the other Apache were scattering. Giff saw one strike the water and then another. He scraped his forearm across his eyes to clear his vision. That's when he saw Jessica Starbuck and the samurai. Ki was using a crazy looking bow with deadly effectiveness, and Jessie was proving that she knew how to handle a Winchester better than most men.

Giff grinned as the surviving Apache broke and raced away. There sure weren't as many as there had been less than thirty minutes ago. He tried to raise his arm and wave but the shoulder was numb, so he just paddled slowly toward shore. A dead Apache floated past him and disappeared around a bend in the river.

Giff crawled up onto the muddy east bank and rolled over onto his back as waves of pain washed over him. He supposed he was in pretty bad shape with the bullet in his shoulder. It would have to come out if there was any chance of surviving. Well, maybe Jessie could do that too. The woman was full of surprises. Giff thought how nice it would be to be Jessie's patient until his shoulder healed, but the pleasant vision died when he thought about his father and the empty saddle covered with blood.

There was no time for recovering from any damned bullet. He was out of time and wanted either to get well quick or die quick and be done with it. Pa was in trouble and had been for a long while now. Giff heard the splashing of a horse being run through water. A moment later, Jessie was kneeling in the mud at his side.

"You damn fool!" she said angrily as she cradled his head in her lap. "Why didn't you let us help you?"

Giff felt very sleepy. He looked up into Jessie's face. Even though her hair was stringy and she was covered with mud, she looked beautiful. "I didn't know you and the samurai could shoot that straight," he managed to whisper. "If I'd known that, *we'd* have been the ones to attack, not them."

Jessie sniffled and touched his cheek. "You did a brave thing trying to act like a decoy. And I don't know about all the other things that are being said about you and your father. All I know is that you're a good man to ride the river with, Giff Jones."

He wanted to tell her thanks, but no words came—only sleep.

They took Giff into Spur the same way that they had earlier taken him into El Paso—across the back of a horse. Jessie had never been to Spur, but she knew that, being this far out on the frontier, it would not be much of a settlement. However, she was not prepared for what she saw. "It's nothing," she said, shading her eyes and staring at the small stockade, and some shacks and dilapidated buildings that emerged in the distance.

Ki nodded. "I'm surprised that the Apache haven't wiped it out yet."

Jessie took a deep breath and expelled it very slowly. "Maybe they have, Ki. Do you see anything moving? Anything at all?"

"No," the samurai decided. "I'm afraid you might be correct. So what do we do now?"

"We have to go there and hope that Giff recovers before the Apache return."

"What about his father?"

Jess just shrugged. She had no idea what to do about Semus Jones and his Texas Rangers. Up until this very moment, she had thought that the people at Spur would be able to provide her with some idea of where the Texas Rangers had vanished. Maybe someone had even found old Semus's body or seen him ride through town on the way back toward Texas. Something! Now, she faced the reality that she and Ki had reached a dead-end trail. And maybe a death trap.

Ki must have been thinking along those same lines because the samurai chose an arrow from his quiver. He nocked the arrow and rode on ahead, his eyes squinting into the sun and yet missing nothing. He noticed that the stockade gates had been busted and now hung askance on their leather hinges. Inside the gates, they could see burned buildings and nothing more.

The samurai rode through the gates and saw that the stockade and the mining offices were all destroyed. Papers were strewn across the ground along with clothes and eating utensils. A box of picks and shovels had been smashed open and then abandoned. Every window in every building not burned to the ground was broken, and at the far end of the compound there had obviously been a huge bonfire. Ki saw the remains of several slaughtered mules.

He turned around in his saddle and waved Jessie forward. This place gave him a bad feeling. There were blackened bones in the ashes of the bonfire and he would bet almost anything that there were human bones scattered among those that had belonged to the mules. Who could tell? Maybe some of them belonged to old Semus Jones and his missing Texas Rangers.

"Let's get him inside, then see if they've poisoned the well," Jessie said, helping the samurai drag Giff off the Indian pony. They carried the unconscious man into one of the buildings that had not been torched. They laid Giff on a

115

table and Jessie ripped open his shirt and studied the wound. "It's not too bad," she said. "I just wish it had passed out the back and we didn't have to go through with this. There isn't even any whiskey to dull the pain."

Ki understood. The Apache would have been looking for three things: weapons, food, and whiskey. "I can help," Ki said, placing his thumb once more on the *atemi* point.

"Are you sure that you won't . . ."

"What?" Ki asked. "Kill him? Of course not. Right now, he's barely out, but I'll put him down a little deeper after I've found you a bucket of water."

"I'll need the use of your *tanto* knife," Jessie said. "I think that the bullet is probably so deep that I'd better go in from the back. With luck, the slug will be just under the surface."

Ki went and tested the water in the well. It tasted brackish, but he could detect no poisoning. With the Rio Grande less than a mile away, there was little point in such an act. The samurai filled an oaken bucket and carried it into the building. He knew that it would be better if they boiled the water, but smoke would be an open invitation for trouble. They had not killed all the Apache back at the river. Some had escaped and would almost certainly go for reinforcements. If a big Apache camp were within a day's ride, Ki knew that the end was near unless they threw Giff back across a saddle or built a travois and tried to drag him to Las Cruces.

Jessie would not do that, so Ki did not waste thought on the possibility. He handed Jessie his knife, then used *atemi* to send the wounded man into deeper unconsciousness. "Do you need me? I'd like to keep watch just in case."

"No," Jessie said. "Just help me roll him over on his stomach and I'll take care of it. This won't be the first, nor probably the last, bullet I dig out of a man."

116

Ki nodded. Jessie had taken several out of him over the last few years. She was far more skilled than the average frontier surgeon, and she knew exactly what she was doing. "I'll be close by," he said, leaving them alone.

As soon as he was gone, Jessie took a deep breath and made an incision in the back of Giff's shoulder. It bled profusely but she used some clean linen she had found as bandages. Within a few tense moments, she felt the blade of Ki's knife scrape something. From experience, she guessed it to be the lead slug she was hunting. Wishing for forceps and doing the best she could without them, she dug down a little and used the tip of the knife to lever the slug out of Giff's shoulder. She let the wound bleed a little more in order to carry out any lead fragments or infection. Then she applied pressure to the shoulder and fashioned a bandage just like she had once seen her father's personal physician apply on a man down in Houston.

Jessie was finished. When she looked up, she was surprised to see that it was well into the afternoon. Shadows were lengthening across the ravaged compound. This place gave her the shivers. She felt the ghosts of many dead men and she knew that she could not escape it fast enough.

How many days before Giff would be well enough to travel? Ki had probably already thought of making a travois. That was not a bad idea except that the mesquite was so thick and heavy that the poles would constantly be bumping over it and causing Giff great pain.

And what about Semus and the other Texas Rangers? Had they died here with the poor, foolish miners? Jessie figured that Ki would be trying to answer that question by careful investigation of the compound. Maybe he'd find a blackened Ranger badge among the bones. Or some other clue.

Jessie sat down wearily on the porch and cradled her

117

head in her hands. She was sick and tired, sick of the killing and tired of dead-ends that led her no closer to resolving the questions and fate of Captain Semus Jones. Why wouldn't Giff be honest with her? If he truly believed that his father was innocent, why didn't he explain? What could he be hiding, and how could she discover the real truth?

Questions and more questions and damn few answers. The only good thing about all this was that she did not have to make excuses to Captain Ben Ray in Austin. Not yet, at least. After traveling for hundreds of difficult miles and maybe getting themselves boxed into a death-trap, she did not know much more than Ben. If anything, the mystery only deepened. Jessie felt as if she had failed completely so far. Maybe Ki would find something to help.

But then again, maybe the damned Apache were on their way back to finish their bloody work.

Chapter 12

Captain Semus Jones knew he had become old when it took him three tries to get the toe of his boot through his stirrup and then heave himself up and into the saddle. He was nearly seventy and looked every day of it. His hair was snow white, as were his mustache and eyebrows. He moved slowly and his bones ached after riding for more than a day and a night. He suffered from the heat, the cold, and hangovers much more than he had in his youth, and he knew that he was getting crotchety and occasionally forgetful.

It was this last curse that bothered him most of all. A man would get old and suffer physically, but he had no legitimate right to complain. After all, being old and aching was still one hell of a lot better than being dead. But it was the mental slippage that bothered the old Ranger captain most of all and worried him increasingly. There were times when it seemed as if he could recall everything that ever happened in his lifetime. Specific gunfights engaged in more than a half-century ago. Faces of men he'd killed, their expressions of shock at the impact of his bullet or the cut of a rope into the flesh of their necks. And women. Semus had had a lot of beautiful women, both brown and white. He'd even had an Apache girl whose life he'd saved. Yes, he could remember the women very well. Their little playful characteristics as well as their special lovemaking techniques. None of them were the same; each was a treasured memory. But more and more, dammit, he was getting to the point where the day-to-day details of life were becoming harder to remember.

Sometimes he even forgot whether or not he'd shaved until he rubbed his jaw. He forgot when he'd cleaned his rifle last or had his horse shod. And now, after weeks in the field, he had forgotten the name of the woman that he had already lost three men trying to rescue.

Semus glanced over at Bud Meeker, the last and probably the best of the Rangers who had left El Paso with him. Bud was riding a black mare that had not proven itself on this long, grueling chase. The mare was skin and bone and ready to drop. Bud knew this, and it had made him sullen. A Ranger on a half-dead horse was in serious trouble.

"Bud?"

"Yeah?"

"What's that woman's name again?"

"Jesus Christ! You asked me that about a hundred times since last week."

Semus bristled with anger and humiliation. "And I'll ask a hundred more damn times and you had better give me an answer," he snapped. "Now what in the hell is her name?"

"Mrs. Marilyn Childs," Bud snapped. "She's the sister of the wife of the mayor of Las Cruces and you swore on your word of honor that you'd bring her back alive from the Apache. It was a fool promise to make, Semus. A damn fool promise to make. Cost us three good men, and our turn might be next. You're too old for this and I know I'm in way over my head. With Billy, Jed, and Mike, we had a chance, but with just the two of us, we're roasted meat for the Apache."

"Aw, bullshit! We're Texas Rangers and there's a woman to bring back alive," Semus told the man. "And while I might be old and getting ornerier by the minute, I can damn sure still hit what I shoot at. My eyes are as good as yours."

"The hell they are!"

Semus spat tobacco. "About three hundred miles straight ahead I see a mesa. Big son of a bitch with steep sides and a tree with a damned sparrow sitting in its branches. No wait, two damn sparrows. See 'em?"

Bud sighed. He leaned forward in his saddle and squinted. "Yeah, yeah, I seen em! Purty little suckers, ain't they?"

Semus held back a grin. "Yeah they are, Bud. And all this just goes to prove that you're just as full of rat-shit as I am."

The two Texas Rangers rode on in silence, each satisfied that he had gotten the better of the other. Presently, Bud stopped his horse and dismounted. "Look at this."

Semus decided not to dismount. He bluffed because he couldn't see a damned thing until Bud climbed back into the saddle. "It's just one Apache footprint. But he's heading right up into that low range of mountains, and they're the same ones you said you figured they'd have their camp in. Maybe we've finally found her."

Semus had already forgotten the woman's name again. "I just hope there's enough of them to make a fair fight of it this time," he grunted.

Bud did not laugh. They had already fought a six-mile running battle with a large force of Apache; that's when they'd lost Billy, Jed, and Mike. Bud knew that it was about half luck that he and Semus had managed to escape with their lives. And if it wasn't for the fact that he could never live with himself if he abandoned the old Ranger captain, Bud figured he'd have turned his horse around and headed back to Texas. He wasn't earning $37.50 a month to kill Apache in New Mexico.

Bud stopped his horse. "How do we play this if they're up there, Semus?"

"We wait until dark and steal into their camp and get her," the old Ranger said, as if there was nothing at all to the task.

Bud shook his head. "Just like that, huh?"

"That's right."

Semus rode over to the shade of some tall mesquite and climbed stiffly down from the saddle. He audibly groaned and then collapsed in a pile. "We ride out an hour after sundown. Wake me when it's time to go."

"I'm halfway inclined to run out on you. If you close your eyes and start to snoring again, you might just wake up and it'll be tomorrow morning. I'll be halfway back to Texas and you'll be staring up at a bunch of damned Apache."

"Life is full of twists," Semus told the man as he pulled his hat over his eyes and fell into a deep, dreamless sleep.

"Wake up, Semus. It's time to ride."

Semus roused himself and climbed heavily to his feet. He unbuttoned his trousers and passed water in slow spurts. It was hell getting old; even his water-pipe was starting to rust out. He felt worse than when he had lain down hours ago but he knew that the sleep would serve him well before the night was over. He glanced over at Bud, who sat waiting patiently on his horse. He wondered if the Ranger had also slept and doubted it. There were dark circles under Bud's eyes and he looked half-starved.

Semus tightened his cinch and made a clumsy job of getting back on his horse, much to Bud's amusement. "I swear, Cap'n, you look like a fat lady trying to mount a camel."

"Go to hell," Semus grunted.

"We're already there, in case you haven't noticed."

There was no more talk after they headed out toward the pine-covered mountains. They rode steadily until after midnight. When they smelled the smoke of a campfire, they dismounted and tied their horses. "Cap'n," Bud said in a low tone of voice, "I sure wish you'd stay here and let me go in alone. No disrespect, but you don't move as quietly as you once did."

Semus bristled with anger. "You can go in for her, but I'll be damned if I'll wait here while you do it. I'll stick close; and if they wake up, I'll lay down a covering fire."

Semus slipped his Winchester from its saddle scabbard. "Now come on!" he hissed impatiently.

They sneaked up to the edge of the camp and crouched down in the trees. With a low fire and the moonlight there was pretty good vision and it was easy enough to see the sleeping figures. "Do you see her?" Bud whispered.

Semus didn't answer until he actually could see the woman, whatever her damned name was. She had been roped to a tree. Her arm was sticking out toward its trunk. "There," Semus whispered.

Bud nodded. "I'll go around to the other side and cut her free. With luck, we'll be twenty miles away before it's dawn and they take up our trail."

But the old Ranger was not pleased. "They're kidnappers and murderers. We ought to kill 'em all, Bud!"

"And risk the life of the woman? Come on, Cap'n. She'd be the first to die, and then Billy, Jed, and Mike would have cashed in their chips for no reason."

Semus fumed but he knew that it was true. "All right,

get her loose and bring her around to the horses. Don't try for one of their ponies or we'll wake 'em for sure."

"Right," Bud said. "If we can make our way back to Spur before they catch us, we've got a chance."

"A damn small chance; them miners can't shoot worth beans," Semus growled in a low undercurrent of voice. "Go on, now!"

Semus watched as Bud moved off into the dark trees. He smelled the smoke and the cooked meat, and he realized that he had not eaten fresh meat in almost two weeks, except for the rabbits and the rattlesnakes they had killed with rocks and nooses. Out in this country, if you fired a shot you never knew what would fire right back at you. His stomach growled so loudly that he was afraid it would wake a sleeping Apache.

Bud stepped up to the girl. Semus could see only his outline as he crouched down beside the girl. Semus held his breath and thought, *cover her mouth tight before you do one other damn thing 'cause she's gonna yell. That's the first thing she'll do, Bud.*

Bud did cover the woman's mouth. A few moments later, when they both stood up and Semus saw Bud and the woman disappear back into the trees, he breathed a heavy sigh of relief. Bud was one of the best. He fussed and worried a lot, but he was a Texas Ranger from the crown of his head to the under-slung heels of his cowboy boots.

Semus hurried back to the horses. He outweighed Bud by a good twenty pounds, but his horse was in much better condition. "Here," he whispered to the Ranger, "you and the woman ride my horse and I'll ride yours."

"What the hell are you talking about!" Bud hissed in anger.

Semus grabbed him by the shoulder and his fingers bit into the man's flesh. "I'm talking about giving orders and taking orders. I'm on the givin' end, you're on the takin' end! Now do as I tell you!"

Bud reluctantly did as ordered. Semus struggled into his saddle and they rode their backtrail down the long, sloping contour of land toward the Rio Grande and the town of Spur. The woman was pretty, but she had obviously been ill-used, and her face and arms showed bruises so plain that Semus could see them even in the moonlight.

When they had ridden a few miles, Semus said, "My name is Captain Jones and this is Ranger Bud Meeker. We're sorry that we took so long to catch up to you, ma'am."

"It don't matter," she said. "I knew you were coming. I always knew the Texas Rangers were coming. You see, I saw 'em run your other friends down and scalp them. The Apache celebrated and showed me the scalps and their Ranger badges. Showed them all to me, and I got sick. But that told me you were coming, and I just had to hold on to myself and wait. I knew you'd never let your friends die for nothing. Even if there were only two of you left, I knew you'd find a way to save my life."

Semus nodded, feeling proud that someone had had more faith in him than he'd had in himself lately. But he was not surprised at the woman's words. This almost blind faith in the Texas Rangers was quite common. The stories were legendary about how a Texas Ranger never quit the trail of an outlaw band of Indians carrying off slaves.

Bud had other thoughts. "I just hope we have enough time to get a ten or fifteen mile lead before they wake up. With us riding double, we'll need all of it, Semus. Every single foot of distance we can gain right now will count for plenty by mid-morning."

Semus knew that Bud was right. He gauged it was about fifty miles to Spur as the buzzards flew. He also figured that they would need more like a twenty-mile head start before day broke and the Apache took up their trail. Semus used his spurs on Bud's sorry horse and wished he were riding his own. Beside him, the woman hung on tight as they began to gallop. Her skirts worked to reveal the calves of her legs and Semus noticed that they were also badly bruised. He wondered how much of her body under her dress was bruised like that. Probably all of her. The Apache would have sold her to the Comancheros, who would have taken her down into Mexico and found a rich, fat landowner who had a craving for gringo women. She'd have been worth quite a lot of money, being yellow-haired, tall, and slender. But she'd have had one hell of a bad life, and probably would have died in a few years.

They galloped for three miles. Finally, it was Bud's horse, not his own carrying two riders, that gave out. Semus pulled the animal in to a stumbling walk. He shook his head. "Bud, do you think that my horse can carry three?" It was a bad joke, and it fell flat.

Bud looked damned worried. "Not too likely. He's about to quit on you, Semus."

"If he does, I want my horse back," the old Ranger said, not meaning a word of it.

But Bud didn't catch the wink of his eye and said hotly, "Hell, take him now!" he said, reining to a standstill.

Semus got angry. "You put a boot on the ground I'll put a bullet through it, dammit! I was just funnin' ya and you had to get sore."

"I ain't in no mood for funnin', Semus. We're in serious trouble and you know it. If that horse can't go on, someone is going to get caught and skewered by the Apache. And since it's my horse, it ought to be me."

Semus spurred the failing horse into a staggering trot just to prove that the animal still had a few more miles left in it before it collapsed. "When this sorry son of a bitch of yours quits, then I'll be the one that stays behind and if that's pullin' rank on you again, then the hell with it!"

Bud clenched his teeth and followed along in silence.

The horse gave out right at sunrise. It just stopped and keeled over dead. Semus had enough time to kick out of the stirrups and land on his feet just as if he were a young man again and nothing in life was hard. In anticipation of the horse's fall, he'd already pulled his Winchester, and now, as he stood beside the animal, he watched the sun hump its way over the eastern horizon.

"I've lived well and long," he said, more to himself than to the pair who sat on his horse, bathed in the golden glow of the morning. "Do you know what I've always been most afraid of, Bud?"

Bud couldn't bring himself to speak. Despite all the rumors about Semus being corrupted by Antonio Castillo, Bud loved and revered this old man. Like every other Ranger stationed in El Paso, he did not understand what possible business Semus could have with such a scumbag as Castillo. Yet he knew that they did do business together. And if Semus took money for favors, then he had either buried it or sent it somewhere, because he sure never spent it on himself.

Semus sat down on the dead horse and crossed his leg over his knee. He looked almost comical, as if he were waiting for a haircut on the boardwalk in front of an El Paso barbershop. "I was always afraid of having a stroke and winding up so paralyzed that I couldn't use a gun to put myself out of my misery. Remember old John Baylor? He was a bull of a man when he siezed up and couldn't move nothing but his eyes. He just lay in bed for months, staring out the window of the boardinghouse. The woman that took care of John hated the job so bad I sort of had to chip in a few dollars a week just so she'd keep him until the end. He messed all over hisself like a baby."

Semus visibly shuddered at the thought. "I watched John sort of shrivel up like a dead animal left in the sun a few months. I was never more scared of anything in my life than witherin' slow like that."

He looked up at the young Ranger. "I think I'm damn lucky to have things work out this way. You know I didn't have many more years to live and I can't think of a better way to go than fighting Apache."

When Bud just nodded bleakly, Semus said, "I want to scribble a note to my son, Giff. You see that he gets it if you and the woman reach El Paso."

"I will."

"Good." Semus reached into his pocket and brought out a pencil and the notepad he had always carried to write down clues and thoughts as they came to him. He laid the pad down on his knee, bent over it and licked the pencil lead, then began to write. He wrote for almost ten minutes, which was about as long as he'd ever written in his life. When he was done, he counted five little pages and was pleased. He folded them up and dropped his cocked boot to the ground. His leg had gone to sleep from the knee down, and he hobbled a little as he stepped over to the Ranger and handed him the note. "I appreciate this, Bud."

"Aw, Jesus Christ," Bud swallowed. "Cap'n, I . . ."

"You and this woman got a long way to go yet. You ride like hell. If you make it to Spur, get them dumb-assed miners to set up for a fight. I'll take out as many Apache as I can, but there'll be a passel that get by me. So long."

The woman reached down from his horse and touched his face. "I will never forget you, mister. Not ever in all my life, I won't."

"Sure you will, and you ought to, ma'am." Semus

raised his hand and said, "Hang on tight; this horse can run a little."

He brought the flat of his hand down across his horse's rump and the animal bolted forward. Bud couldn't look back because of the woman hanging onto his belt. But the woman did look back after a few moments, and when she did, she saw that the old Texas Ranger had retaken his place on the dead horse and had lit himself a cigar. The woman closed her eyes and let silent tears stream down her bruised cheeks.

The Apache came two-and-a-half hours later. They came fast, and they were in a murdering mood. The captive woman had been a great prize, and she would have brought much money from the Comanchero. Because of her youth and beauty, she might even have been sold to one of the Apache chiefs. Now she was gone and, even worse, they had suffered the humiliation of having two men boldly sneak right into their camp!

When they first saw the old Texas Ranger, he was standing beside his fallen horse with his rifle resting across his chest. He was still for so long as they galloped nearer that he seemed dead. He didn't run or take cover behind the body of the horse or seem to do anything. They knew that dead men did not stand upright, and so the Apache spread out into a skirmish line and drew their rifles or nocked arrows on their bowstrings. They would kill this one quickly and waste no time in overtaking the other man and the white woman slave. Yet there was something very noble about the lone white man standing to face his death, and each warrior hoped that he would be the one to kill the man and take his scalp. True, it was gray and not as impressive as that of a young man. But when the story of how the old one had stood to face them alone was told, the scalp would receive good honor.

Semus waited until they were a hundred yards away and then he lifted his rifle to his shoulder and started shooting their horses. He dropped six of them before the first Apache bullet knocked him down. He pushed himself into a sitting position and shot three more horses, knowing this was the way he could best slow them down and give Bud and the woman a chance of reaching Spur. Semus tried to stand again as the Apache swept in on him, their faces alive with hatred, only his legs had no strength. And then they were on top of him and he was falling. But instead of hitting the ground, he fell until sunrise was replaced by the darkness of an eternal night.

Chapter 13

While Jessie had spent most of her first day at Spur taking care of Giff Jones, Ki had worked from morning to night to repair the big wooden gates that had been broken by the Apache. By using a stout ten-foot pine pole as a pry bar, he had leveraged the heavy gates into position, then replaced the leather hinges. He had also repaired the walls and done whatever he could to make the stockade more defensible. But Ki knew that if the Apache came in force they were all doomed. Even if Giff was able to use a gun effectively, the perimeter of the stockade was simply too long to defend. He remembered reading that the same had been true of the Alamo. Had the mission walls not enclosed such a huge area to defend, the outcome for Colonel Travis, Crockett, Bowie, and the others might well have been far different.

Ki walked into the cabin that Jessie had chosen to use as an infirmary and a place to live until Giff was strong enough to travel. Giff was sitting up in bed, but he was pale and it was clear that the loss of blood had left him very weak. "How are you feeling?" he asked.

Giff managed a grin. "Thanks to Jessie and you, I'll live to fight again. In fact, I've been telling Jessie that we ought to get out of here right now. Those Apache that got away will be coming back with a passel of friends. They'll want revenge and we sure aren't in any shape to hold them off."

"You're not fit to travel," Jessie argued. "If you try to

leave today, that bullet wound will open up and you'll likely bleed to death."

"There are some worse ways of dyin', Jessie. And if the Apache come back, we'll learn a couple of them first-hand." The man looked at Ki with pleading eyes. "Talk some sense into her, Ki."

"I'm sorry," Ki said. "She doesn't listen to anyone."

"All right," Jessie said. "We'll leave tonight. Ki, why don't you make a travois and—"

"Whoa!" Giff said. "I'm riding out of here on a horse, not being bounced and dragged along behind one."

It was clear to Jessie by the tone of the big man's voice that there would be no compromise on this issue. "All right," she said once more, "but if you lose consciousness, we'll just have to tie you across the saddle."

Giff nodded. "I just need a little rest, is all," he said. "I'll be plenty ready for gettin' out of here tonight. There's only one thing that hurts and that's not finding out what happened to my pa and those other Rangers. Every one of them was a friend, and I'd hate to think they went down to the Apache somewhere around here. If they did, I'd at least want to find what's left of 'em and give them a decent burial."

"I know that," Jessie said. "But this isn't the time. Besides, maybe . . . well, maybe they're back in El Paso right now, wondering what the devil could have happened to us. Think about that."

"I'd like to," Giff said, "but it doesn't seem likely, and—"

Ki whirled out of the room and sprinted to the wall, where he climbed up on the parapet and shouted, "There's a man and a woman riding double! And they're being chased by at least twenty Apache!"

"Maybe it's your father," Jessie said as she grabbed her rifle and headed outside.

Giff pushed himself out of bed. When he stood up, his head spun. He could hear distant firing, and the dizziness in his head passed after a moment. He pulled his boots on, grabbed his cartridge belt, and strapped it onto his hip. He remembered that he had lost both his rifles in the Rio Grande and he cussed with fury. A sixgun wasn't much use against an Indian attack, but it was the best he could do this time. Feeling light in the head, he navigated his way outside into the late afternoon sun. His shoulder began to throb, but the pain only sharpened his senses. When he came to the stockade gate, he peered through the cracks to see Ranger Bud Meeker riding like hell with a tall, yellow-haired woman holding on for dear life.

Ki was already pulling the gate open and with Giff's help they swung it just wide enough for the faltering horse to shoot into the stockade. Ki and Giff threw the gate shut, and the samurai sprang back up on the parapet. Since the Apache were still out of effective handgun range, Giff watched as the samurai took an arrow from a quiver and nocked his strange looking bow. Ki waited almost a full minute until the Apache were in his range; then the samurai drew the bowstring back to his ear and, without seeming to aim, he fired. Giff was amazed to see that the bow turned completely around. When the ex–Texas Ranger peered through the gate again, he saw that the arrow had buried itself in an Apache's chest. The man was tumbling from his horse. It was an incredible display of marksmanship and, had things not been so damned dicey, Giff would have shouted congratulations. But that could come later.

Bud Meeker came running up beside Giff, a rifle clenched tightly in his hands.

"You look like hell," Giff said, wanting to ask Bud

133

about Semus but realizing that there was no time for questions now.

"I've been through hell," Bud gritted, poking his rifle through the gap between the gates and taking aim. He fired but missed. "And so has the woman I brought back. I better get up on the parapet with that crazy Chinaman with the bow and that pretty woman. You sure pick strange company to get yourself scalped with."

"He's a samurai," Giff corrected, "and if you don't get yourself killed in the next few minutes, you're going to discover that both he and the woman are fightin' fools."

Bud and Giff went up to join Jessie and Ki, who were both very glad to see help arrive. "The Apache have turned back," Jessie said as she reloaded.

Bud nodded. "They lost three men, and that's enough to make them want to rethink the situation. My guess is that they'll regroup and decide to wait until dark."

Jessie had been thinking the same thing. "Any chance of us slipping away before they come?"

The Texas Ranger nodded. "In my humble opinion, miss, that is our only chance."

Jessie watched the Apache regroup out of rifle range. She hurriedly counted at least two dozen. "You know Apache better than we do, Ranger. Is there any chance they might just give up the fight and go away?"

"Nope."

Jessie waited a few minutes longer. When it became obvious that the Apache were not going to make another charge at the gate, she climbed down from the parapet and went to the woman, who stood looking very frightened and battered. "There's food inside," Jessie said. "Are you hungry?"

The woman shook her head. "What I most want is to

wash away the smell of them," she whispered. "Can I do that?"

"Of course." Jessie took her arm. The woman did smell of blood and other things that Jessie did not even want to think about. Her dress was nothing but a filthy rag, torn and caked with grease and dirt. "I saw a tin washtub, and the well water is good if you don't mind it being cold. I found a bit of soap and there are some men's clothes you can wear if you want to change."

Marilyn Childs nodded gratefully. "When I was with them, I sometimes thought that if I could wash away... everything, then I wouldn't go crazy. I hope that is true."

Jessie took her inside and gently sat her down in a chair. "I'll go and get the tub and some water. The soap is right over there on the counter, and I'll have Ki find some clean clothes for you if it looks as if he won't be needed up on the wall."

"Oh, I pray they'll go away and leave us in peace!" the woman breathed passionately. "I've already seen enough killing to last me a lifetime. It broke my heart when Captain Jones stayed behind and gave his own life to save ours."

Jessie turned quickly. "He was alive?"

"Until this morning, very much so. He was the bravest man I ever knew. Old and brave and kind. He's the reason me and that other Ranger are here now. The only reason."

Jessie hid her reaction well. She had quit her roundup over a month ago in order to solve the mystery of why Semus Jones had taken up with Antonio Castillo. Now, it appeared that she might never know the reasons behind the Ranger captain's apparent corruption. Maybe it was for the best, yet she could only imagine what Giff must be going through.

Jessie walked to the door and peered across the compound to see both Giff and the Texas Ranger standing face to face. The Ranger handed Giff a little wad of folded papers and placed his hand on Giff's shoulder. Suddenly, Giff turned away quickly and moved off to be by himself. As she watched him unfold the papers and read the note she assumed was left by his father, no one had to tell Jessie that he had just been told about his father's tragic end. Giff's ruggedly handsome face seemed to crumple with pain, and Jessie felt her heart go out to the man. It was obvious that Giff had loved his father deeply and would miss him very much in the years to come. Jessie found herself wishing she had known old Semus Jones better. The Texas Ranger captain had been a man around whom legends were made, and yet somehow he had gone bad at the very end of his career. Jessie was sure that Antonio Castillo must have had some kind of hold over Semus; the old Texas Ranger would never have consorted with an outlaw in order to fatten his own bank account.

No, Jessie thought, *I may never find out what caused Semus to go bad, but I would bet my ranch that it was something of vital importance*. Jessie thought that observation might be worth something to Captain Ray back in Austin.

I had better go for that tub and the bathwater, she thought to herself. Jessie shaded her eyes and looked up at the samurai, who stood like a sentinel against the bright blue sky. He would stand there for hour after hour, unmoving, seeing everything until darkness fell, darkness that would certainly bring the Apache. They had stormed these rickety walls once already and slaughtered the Spur miners. They'd do it again even faster. This stockade was a death-trap, and as far as Jessie was concerned she would much rather make a stand somewhere out on the plains than be trapped and cornered like rats in a cage.

Yes, she thought, hauling up a bucket of cool water for the woman inside, *we'll make a run for it, even though we are one horse short. And with luck, we might even live to see El Paso once again.*

The sun slipped behind the stark western hills and the tortured land seemed to heave a sigh of relief. The temperature dropped appreciably and they watched the shadows of distant hills stretch across a sea of gray mesquite. Jessie walked up to Giff, who stood beside his horse. He was fumbling with the latigo and trying to tighten his cinch, with only limited success.

"It's a little easier with two hands," Jessie said, helping him.

"Yeah," he replied quietly.

"Giff, I'm sorry about your father. Marilyn told me how he sacrificed his own life to save her and Bud. And you used yourself as a decoy and tried to save Ki and me. Bravery must run in the Jones family blood."

Giff turned to face her. "I want you to know something, Jessie. I want you to know that my father left a letter for me explaining why he worked with Antonio Castillo and sometimes looked the other way on things."

"It's done," Jessie said quickly. "Your father was a hero. I don't want to hear about his failings. That's history now."

But Giff shook his head. "No. It's not history. And it won't be over until you tell Captain Ray back in Austin what happened."

Jessie shook her head. "We might not even live through the next few hours. Why don't you tell me if we do."

"Because I need to tell you now!" he rasped. "You see, I never could figure it out why Pa was in cahoots with Castillo, either. It just kept eating and eating at me until I knew I had to quit the Rangers and get out or I was going to start

137

killing like an animal that has gone totally bad. I begged Pa to tell me why he dealt with Castillo but he never would say. Not until this letter."

Jessie waited knowing he was going to answer the same question that she had been agonizing over ever since she'd talked to Captain Ray in Austin.

In his typical fashion, Giff minced no words but instead plunged right to the heart of the matter. "Castillo knows where my half-sister is being held as a slave in Mexico."

Jessie frowned. "Slow down a little. You have a half-sister?"

Giff nodded. "Yeah. You see, my real mother died when I was a baby. Pa eventually found a Mexican woman whose name was Rubenita to take care of me and . . . well, over the years he came to love her. He never married the woman because there was just something in him that said a man was never supposed to have more than one wife in a lifetime. But he loved Rubenita and she gave him a daughter, my half-sister. Maria was only six years old when the Apache came. Pa and I were away at the time, and when we returned, Rubenita was dead. And even though Father searched and searched, he could never find out what happened to Maria. Eventually, he came to believe that she was dead or lost somewhere deep in Mexico. But somehow, Antonio Castillo found out where Maria is living and that she is alive and well, though she is a virtual slave to a rich and powerful official down in Mexico."

Jessie leaned forward and saw how the pieces of the puzzle were starting to fit in place.

Giff continued. "Castillo knows—or at least convinced Pa he knew—where Maria was being kept. He swore that as long as Pa helped him, he'd see that Maria was treated well. But if he refused, she would suffer."

Jessie just shook her head in wonder. "How could he just take the word of a man like Antonio Castillo as the truth?"

"Castillo has guts," Giff said. "He's also very persuasive, and perhaps he showed Pa something of Maria's, a ring or a toy. It must have been enough to convince Pa that his daughter was still alive. Anyhow, the note says that they made a deal. Five years of betrayal to the Texas Ranger oath in exchange for their lives."

Giff expelled a deep breath. "My pa was wrong, Jessie. But what is done is done. Now I have to find a way to locate Maria and save her."

"Mexico is huge," Jessie said. "Your sister could be anywhere down there."

"I know that, and so did Pa. He said to start with Castillo. Torture him to death if necessary in order to find out the truth. And I'll do that. I won't hesitate a minute. Maria will be twenty now. She'll be forced into marriage or worse, if she hasn't been already. If a man has violated my sister, I will kill him for sure."

The way he said it made Jessie shudder. "I want to help you find Maria," she said.

"No."

"You can't stop me from helping," Jessie said. "I've gotten in too deep to just walk away from this now. Besides, Castillo cannot be trusted. The entire story might be fabricated."

"My father would not have helped him if he hadn't been dead certain that Maria was still alive," Giff said stubbornly.

"I hope that's true," Jessie said quietly. "But we can't be certain."

Giff looked at her and then at the last fading color of

day. "If we live to see sunrise, we can talk about it tomorrow," he said.

Jessie nodded. That was fair enough. Before they could even begin to think about saving Maria Jones, they had to think about saving themselves.

Chapter 14

Jessie looked up at the moon and wished it wasn't so damned bright. There was no way that they could hope to get out of the stockade without being seen by the Apache, who would immediately take up a pursuit. Right now, however, Ki and Bud had sneaked out into the sagebrush and were busily setting up trip-ropes for the Apache ponies. If they could drop enough Apache ponies, and if they could all reach the river and get across, there might be a chance of escaping.

Giff studied Jessie in the pale moonlight. "I wish you and the Childs woman weren't with us," he said. "It would make me more comfortable."

"I'm glad to be here," Jessie told the man. "I know how to shoot and I'm not afraid of dying if it's my time. I've talked to Marilyn a few minutes ago and she feels the same, though she's never fired a gun before in her life."

"You're a pretty remarkable pair of women. Bud says that Mrs. Childs has a lot of sand. And you're not only brave but beautiful. I'd always figured that those who had the most to lose would be the ones that fought the hardest to save their lives and the least likely to sacrifice them for any reason."

"I don't believe that's a bit true," Jessie said. "I was left with plenty of money, but I sure don't think that entitles me to any better chance at life than someone who is poor."

"Frankly, neither do I," Giff said. "But then, being poor

141

myself, I tend to think along that line. You know, if we get to El Paso, and if you still are of a mind to help me find Maria, I'd like that just fine. And of course, the samurai is worth his weight in gold. Havin' him join us would be icin' on the cake."

"Oh, he'll come along with us," Jessie promised.

They both heard the whistle that was Ki's signal for them to mount up and come to the gate ready to bust out and make a run for the river. Jessie mounted Sun and watched Giff take a position beside the gate in preparation to throwing it open.

"Do we have any chance at all?" Marilyn Childs asked.

"You bet!" Jessie said, hearing the faint thumping sound made by the mallets that Ki and Bud were using to hammer stakes into the earth. Between the stakes they were stretching rope about two feet above the ground. Hopefully, since they were hiding the trip-ropes in the thick mesquite, the ropes would not be seen and would prove extremely effective in slowing their pursuers.

A second low whistle was the signal they had been waiting for. "Here we go," Giff said heaving the gate open just enough to allow their horses to race through. Ignoring the pain in his wounded shoulder, he mounted the Indian pony, then slapped it across the rump and led the charge out through the gates. Marilyn followed Giff on Semus's horse, and Jessie came out last leading Ki's mount.

The Apache saw them at once. They had probably been almost prepared to attack and now were caught slightly off guard. They howled in anger even as Jessie and the others spurred forward. Ki and Bud seemed to rise up from the earth. Bud vaulted onto Semus's horse behind Marilyn, and Ki swung effortlessly onto his own mount.

"Let's go!" Jessie shouted.

No one needed any urging as their horses bolted forward

to run headlong toward the Rio Grande with the Apache in full chase. Jessie glanced back over her shoulder to see a wild scene of falling horses and Indians. There was a huge dust cloud where they tumbled, and as many riderless animals emerged from it as did those with Apache still mounted.

Jessie and Ki stayed close to the others even though, being on superior horses, they could easily have outdistanced everyone. It was a wild and headlong race. Bud and Marilyn were the slowest but even so they seemed to be flying over the sagebrush-covered land. When they finally reached the river, the Indians were still a good two hundred yards behind. Jessie did not allow Sun to break stride as they plowed into the water. In a moment, they were all swimming, and when they reached the far bank, they bailed off their animals, made a skirmish line, and opened fire on the Indians who were starting to come across.

The Apache had already suffered once in the river under fire, and this time they retreated with only two casualties.

"Mount up!" Giff ordered. "If we stay here, they'll flank us."

They all mounted except the samurai. "I'll stay behind," he said. "It's the only chance we have. Bud, you take my horse."

"The hell I will," the Texas Ranger growled. "If anyone stays behind, it'll be me, not you!"

Ki looked up at Jessie. "You know I am *ninja*. I can disappear into the land and they will never see me. I have a river I can follow, fish I can catch. I can survive and meet you in El Paso, Jessie. There is no other way."

Jessie wanted to protest but she knew that Ki was right. He had a good chance of survival while the Texas Ranger would certainly be captured and horribly tortured to death. "All right," she said. "I won't expect to see you for at least two weeks. I don't want you to hurry and take any unnecessary chances. Go slow, Ki. They'll not give up hunting you. Not after you take their measure before disappearing."

"I know that," he said. "Now go quickly!"

"Better do as the samurai says and come along with us, Bud," Giff told his friend. "That man can out-Apache the Apache. You or I would take a few with us, but we'd both end up watching our own feet get roasted in their fire."

Bud knew when he was outvoted. He took Ki's horse and mounted. "So long," he said, extending his hand down to the samurai. "If you get out of this hellish land, I owe you a drink in El Paso."

Ki nodded. He took his bow and weapons and slipped into the sagebrush then vanished from sight.

"You know," Giff said, "I almost feel sorry for the first Indians who cross that river and find him waiting for them."

Jessie reined Sun south. They would follow the Rio Grande right into El Paso, which was still nearly a hundred miles away. But, thanks to Ki, they'd make it. She had to keep telling herself that the samurai would rejoin her and Giff down in Texas and that everything would be fine.

But as they galloped away and she heard the Apache yells and the sounds of their horses striking the river again, Jessie was worried.

Ki waited until the Apache were in the middle of the river before he unleashed his first arrow. It flew straight to its target and knocked an Apache off his horse and into the water. Ki did not aim to kill; rather he aimed to wound his enemy so that other Apache would be forced to halt their pursuit in order to save the lives of their fellow tribesmen. He had six remaining arrows and he used them all with such rapid delivery that the Apache were thrown into total confusion. Several times bullets fired in his direction but always from the back of a plunging Indian pony. When the samurai had depleted his supply of arrows, he dropped back into the sagebrush and started moving rapidly upriver.

He could hear the cries of the wounded Apache and their friends. Ki peered over the bank of the river and saw the Indians pulling their wounded companions out of the river and across the sandy beach to safety in the willows. Ki knew that there would be no more attempts to cross the river in daylight. The Apache would be staring at the samurai arrows with amazement, and they would not be able to understand just who had shot so skillfully. There would be much debate, but in the morning, the remaining Apache warriors would be coming across the river with a vengeance.

Ki knew that he needed to throw them off Jessie's backtrail and lead them north again, into their own country. The Apache would be certain that he was crazy, for no man who entered their land on foot could possibly expect to escape. They would also realize his brave intentions. But they would kill him all the same.

The samurai walked northward along the river's edge for mile after mile, always careful that his tracks could be easily seen by the Apache. But around two o'clock in the morning, he stepped into the river, waded out into its center and let the current take his body and pull it downriver. He held onto his bow and said a little prayer that the river would take him back past the Apache before sunrise. If he were off in his calculations, there was little chance that he would be alive to see another sundown.

Jessie, Bud, Marilyn, and the injured Giff Jones reached El Paso two days later, about eight o'clock in the morning.

They were worn out and their horses were thin and weary, but they were alive and each of them knew it was because of Ki, who had led the Apache off in another direction.

Their arrival in El Paso caused quite a stir, for all of them had been thought dead. Marilyn wasted no time in rejoining her husband, and Jessie hoped that the woman could put her life back together and somehow manage to forget her terrible ordeal as an Apache captive.

"I better get over to the headquarters and relieve old Art," Bud said, obviously a little reluctant to leave Jessie and Giff. "I sure can't tell you how much you helped, Miss Starbuck. And if that samurai of yours really is able to come back here, then . . . ."

"He'll make it," Jessie repeated. "What are you going to say when you telegraph Captain Ray in Austin?"

"Well, Giff here has already asked me not to say anything about that sister of his he thought was dead all these years. So I'll just say that Captain Semus Jones and three damned fine Texas Rangers were killed by the Apache, and that I could sure use some help."

"Thanks," Giff said. "After this is over and I get Maria back, I'll personally ride over and have a talk with Captain Ray. I'll tell him why my pa did what he did."

Bud scratched his stubbled cheek. "I'd like to go across the border and help you pull Castillo up on his toes by his . . . well," he said, realizing that Jessie might be offended by his next few words, "well, anyway, I want to help you take care of Castillo and get your sister back."

"Uh-uh," Giff said. "Whether you realize it or not, Bud, you're the only Ranger in these parts now. The one in command. You've got to stay on this side of the border and play by the rules. Why, they'll probably make you a captain!"

"God help me," Bud said. "I don't want no command. Only a raise in pay."

"You can't have one without the other, my friend."

Bud didn't look pleased. "Well," he said. "There'll be a lot of reports to file and that telegraph to Austin to get off. I better go along now."

"Yeah," Giff said. "Get along."

Bud had one more thing on his mind. "If you get your sister back safe and all this blows over, I want you riding beside me again, Giff. There is none better than you, and it's what you was meant to do. Mustanging will just get you killed. It's too damned rough and dangerous a way to make a living."

Giff chuckled softly. "It's about on the same scale as Rangering, I'd think. But first things first. It's my sister that counts now."

Bud nodded. "I just wanted you to know where I stood on that. *Adios,* and good luck in Old Mexico."

They watched him ride on down the street. "He'll make a great captain," Giff said.

"So will you," Jessie replied.

Giff chose to ignore that comment. "I'll be heading back to my horse ranch for a few days to rest up and get things ready for Mexico," Giff said when he was alone with Jessie. "No sense for me to stick around town."

"What about a doctor?" she asked.

Giff reached out and touched her cheek. "You were doctor enough for me in Spur, Jessie. You're the only one I want to see."

She felt the heat of his eyes blaze into hers and she smiled. "Maybe I'll ride out to your place in a few days and make a house call."

He nodded. "You could come right now if you want."

"No," she said a little reluctantly. "I need a couple days

to get things organized for our trip down into Mexico. I suppose you'll want to go straight after Antonio Castillo for the answers?"

"He's the key," Giff said. "I consider him the one responsible for putting my pa through hell. If the man hadn't had Pa on a string on account of Maria, he'd have been dead a long, long time ago."

Jessie understood. "Have you any food out at your place?"

"Enough," Giff said, remounting the weary Indian pony. "But I guess if you showed up with something for the pot I wouldn't be too upset."

"I'll do that," Jessie promised.

Giff touched spurs to the pony and said, "Two days, Jessie. If you aren't there by then, I'll come looking for you."

Jessie watched Giff ride away: a big, big man on a little stumpy Indian pony. He would be needing time to work out his own grief over the death of his father, and that was the main reason why she had decided not to go with him to his place. That and the fact that she needed to send her Circle Star foreman a telegram to find out if everything was all right and whether the roundup and trail driver were on schedule.

"Excuse me, Miss Starbuck, but my name is Ronald Burt of the El Paso *Times*. I'd like a story on what happened to you and the others up in New Mexico Territory."

Jessie turned to see a man in his forties standing hopefully in wait. "You want a story? One about how a great Texas Ranger captain gave his life to save the lives of a fellow Texas Ranger and Mrs. Childs?"

"Yes, ma'am!"

"Then you'd better talk to Ranger Bud or Mrs. Childs because they were there and I wasn't," Jessie said, turning toward her hotel room and feeling so incredibly weary she wondered if she could sleep for the next twenty-four hours without interruption.

"But Miss Starbuck, you're the one that's rich and famous!" the reporter protested, running up behind her. "I sure would like to hear your side of the story."

Jessie took pity on the man. "I'll tell you what," she said. "Give me a day to rest and recover and I'll give you a story."

"Thank you!"

"You're welcome," Jessie said, handing the newspaper man her reins. "And in return, I know you'll be kind enough to take my horse over to the livery. Tell the stableman to feed and curry him well. Grain him plenty and clean my saddle."

"Surely you're not intending to go off somewhere again. Why, you look worn out, Miss Starbuck."

Jessie shook her head. "The only place I'm going is to get a bath, some food, and lots of sleep. Good night, sir."

He took her reins and tipped his hat. "Good night, Miss Starbuck. I'll come for that story tomorrow mornin' for sure."

Jessie rode out to Giff's little horse ranch two days later. She felt like a new woman, having slept a great deal since her return from Indian country. She was still worried about Ki, but confident that the samurai would return before long to rejoin her.

When she saw Giff again, he was riding a tall chestnut gelding around and around in his breaking pen. The animal was long-limbed and splendidly put together, with a conformation that promised both speed and endurance.

"Where did you get him?" Jessie called to the horseman.

Giff looked over at her and grinned. He had shaved except for his mustache, and the pinched look in his face was gone now. He appeared years younger than he had in New Mexico Territory.

"I got him from a *vaquero* friend of mine who owed me a few favors. I just let him wipe 'em all out with this one gift."

"He's a beauty."

Giff nodded. He reined the horse over to her and said, "I like him because he sort of has the same color hair you do, Jessie."

Before Jessie could quite think of an answer, Giff reached out and pulled her in close so that she was half out of her saddle and half in his. He kissed her full on the lips, and when he was finished, he deposited her back in her saddle and they both dismounted.

"I guess there's no use in going through all the motions and small talk," she said a little breathlessly as she took his big hand and walked with him toward his cabin.

"Not a reason in the world, Jessie." When they entered the cabin, he left the door standing open so there was sunlight streaming into the interior.

Jessie saw a neat but very spartan room. There was the usual rifle rack and pot-bellied stove. A saddle and some other tack lay in a corner behind a small table with two chairs. Against two walls were the beds; one no doubt had been Semus's and the other, which he led her over to, was Giff's.

"I know it isn't very impressive for a woman like yourself," he said as if he suddenly realized how modest his place must seem to a rich woman. "I imagine you have a beautiful house with imported furniture and a bed with silk..."

Jessie kissed him and wrapped her arms around his

neck. "I have a bed with silk sheets," she whispered, "but it doesn't have a big man in it to satisfy me. Does yours, Giff?"

He nodded eagerly. "You bet."

Jessie unbuttoned his shirt and he shrugged out of it. He'd changed the bandage she had made at Spur, and she could tell at a glance that his shoulder wound was healing cleanly and without infection. His chest was covered with a thick mat of hair, and she kissed his nipples until they were hard and she could hear his heart thumbing against his ribcage.

Jessie stepped back and loosed her long hair, which tumbled down to her shoulders. She unbuttoned her own blouse. There was nothing under it but her large and lovely breasts, which swung free.

Giff cupped them in his large, rough hands, and a shiver passed through her body. He bent his head and took one in his mouth and sucked on it until she trembled with eagerness. Then he took the other and did the very same thing until she was clinging to him, fumbling for the buttons on his Levi's, reaching into them and finding his massive rod.

"I don't want to wait long for you," she whispered with urgency.

He eased her down on his bed. He pulled off her boots and spurs, then helped her shuck out of her riding pants. Finally, he slipped her silk underpants off and stood gazing down at her long, slender legs and the beautiful flare of her hips.

"Aren't you even going to bother to shut the door?" she asked as he slowly undressed and stood over her like a sleek animal, his huge rod rising and falling with the beat of his pulse.

"Nope," he said, pushing her legs apart and climbing between them.

Jessie reached down with both of her hands and grabbed his manhood. She began to rub it up and down between her legs, feeling her juices start to flow. He started sucking on her breasts again, and the moment she felt herself ready, she reached around and grabbed his buttocks.

"Now," she hissed between her teeth as she pulled him hard to her and hunched up her hips to accept every ounce of him. "Please go into me now!"

"Yes ma'am!" he said, thrusting his powerful hips forward.

Jessie had had big men before, but none any bigger. Her mouth flew open and her eyes widened with a mixture of momentary pain which almost instantly turned to pleasure as his great hot tool sank into her womanhood and began to move in and out.

"Oh, yes," she moaned, rocking him back and forth inside of her, feeling him begin to move around and around like a giant stirring rod whipping up her passions. "Yes!"

He was so big and experienced that he quickly brought her to the point of no return. She was dimly aware that he was still sucking on her breasts and that his body was in command of her own. She could hear her heart, and her head was spinning as he used her expertly until her legs were waving up in the air. Then she cried out with pleasure, begging him to move even faster.

Giff obliged her in every way. He was on the ragged end of his own control, and when she began to thrash and buck up and down, he knew that she had reached her climax. Giff wanted to meet her halfway. He slammed his root in and out so fast that when she cried out in ecstasy, he roared like a lion and filled her lovely body with great torrents of his hot seed.

Flies were buzzing when Jessie rolled her head weakly toward the door. She saw their horses stomping in the dust as they watched the coupling of their masters. "Look at them watch us," she panted, trying to get her breath. "They must think it's curious."

Giff lifted up on his elbows and looked through the doorway. "Yeah," he breathed a little hoarsely. "And before the day is out, they're going to see a whole lot more!"

Jessie was in no position to argue the fact.

Chapter 15

Because of the boarded up windows and the fact that Giff had closed the door, daylight did not penetrate the cabin. Jessie, weary but satisfied after a wonderful night of lovemaking, did not awaken until late the following afternoon. Even then she might have rolled back over and gone to sleep again except that when she reached for Giff, he was gone. Jessie dozed lightly for almost another hour before she opened her eyes and whispered, "Giff?"

No answer.

She rubbed sleep from her eyes and stretched. She had no idea what time of day it was. Yet it must have been afternoon because she could feel heat seeping in through the cabin walls. Giff must have gone outside to ride the young chestnut gelding or to feed and check on the stock.

Jessie rolled out of bed. She felt a little heavy in the legs, and when she stood up, she had to grope her way to the door. Pushing it open, she was blinded by the light of the late afternoon sun. "Giff?"

No answer.

Jessie closed the door halfway and then moved over to the bed and found her clothes. She dressed and absently combed her hair. She would take a bath before the sun went down, and she'd brought some steaks and food enough to cook them a nice supper. Giff was quite a man, and Jessie could not help but smile at the night they had spent together. She didn't know if she was quite up to another equally as strenuous, but that remained to be seen.

Stepping outside, she shielded her eyes from the sun and looked around the yard. Seeing nothing, not even her own horse, Jessie frowned and called again, "Giff, where are you?"

It was then that she saw the note tacked to the empty horse corral. Feeling a growing sense of uneasiness, Jessie hurried across the yard and read: GONE FOR CASTILLO ALONE. MY FIGHT, NOT YOURS. SORRY. YOUR HORSE IS IN TOWN. GIFF.

Jessie wadded up the note and hurled it to the dirt, then kicked it flying. "Dammit, Giff!" she cried. "You *can't* do it all alone! You'll need help!"

Jessie did not waste a second going back into the cabin. She finished dressing, strapped her sixgun on around her hip, grabbed the apple pie she had brought for them to share, and then marched out the door. She took two steps into the yard, then whirled and went back to lock the door with the huge padlock. She was mad as hell at Giff, and those damn steaks she'd bought for tonight's dinner were going to go to waste. But at least she'd not also waste a perfectly scrumptious looking, fresh apple pie.

Jessie figured that if she stepped out she would be in El Paso by early evening and in Juarez before ten o'clock. Maybe Giff could somehow breach Castillo's walls and security, but she doubted it. The man would have already heard that Captain Semus Jones was dead, and it didn't take a genius to guess that his son would be coming to settle accounts. Antonio Castillo was a very shrewd man. Jessie had charmed him once, and he'd been made a fool of when they'd entered his *casa* and then managed to escape with his young señorita. Castillo would not be tricked so easily again.

156

To Jessie's way of thinking, Giff had little or no chance at all of getting to Castillo and learning the whereabouts of his sister. Jessie headed down the hot and dusty road. She was wearing riding boots that were never designed for walking. By the time she reached El Paso, she figured she'd be half crippled.

Damn that hard-headed Giff Jones! He probably figured he was doing her some big favor by taking her horse so she couldn't catch up with him. Well, he was wrong. And what's more, when she found him down in Mexico hanging by his toes in Castillo's cellar, she would give him a piece of her mind before she bailed him out of the mess he'd gotten himself into.

Giff had left Jessie's palomino in El Paso, then had hurried across the Rio Grande into the busy city of Juarez. He rode tall and loose in the saddle, and when the men who hung around outside the whorehouses and *cantinas* saw him, they fell silent until he passed. Giff ignored the occasional twinge of shoulder pain that sometimes cut through him when he turned too suddenly. He had been thinking about Jessie all afternoon, and now, he guessed, she would be madder than hell at him for taking her horse and forcing her to walk all the way to town.

But he was really doing her a favor. This was his fight, not hers. And she'd already been down here, paid a visit to Don Antonio Castillo, and nearly gotten herself killed. What Jessie didn't seem to realize was that Don Antonio owned the Mexican police and politicians in this town. He contributed generously to all their personal fortunes and had thus collected markers. So if a man got in trouble with Don Antonio, he could expect nothing in the way of assistance from the Mexican authorities.

Giff rode a half-circle around Castillo's hilltop mansion

with its high adobe walls. If it had not been for his half-sister Maria, he would not have had a care in the world this night. He would have figured to kill Castillo and then escaped from Mexico. And if he had failed to escape, then at least he would be exacting sweet revenge on the man who had used his father and soiled the reputation of the Texas Rangers. But with Maria alive somewhere in Mexico, Giff was aware that he had an obligation to at least find and free her from bondage. He realized that there was a good chance that Castillo had lied from beginning to end. Maria might actually be dead, as he and Semus had always supposed. Or she might be perfectly happy somewhere in Mexico. But Giff, like his father, knew he had to find out for himself. To hear it from Maria's very own lips.

He rode the chestnut right up to the adobe wall, and then carefully eased up until he was standing in the saddle. The horse fidgeted and Giff knew he could not afford to hesitate, so he jumped for the top of the thick wall. He caught it, but the effort put a violent strain on his arms and shoulders and he felt the bullet wound tear open. For a moment, he hung against the wall hearing the hoofbeats of his horse recede into the night, Giff was afraid that he would black out and fall helplessly to the ground. If that happened, he would be in a bad fix, bleeding and horseless. Hardly a threat to Castillo.

But he held on until the pain sharpened his senses, and then he slowly hauled his 230 pounds up onto the rim of the wall. The adobe was very warm, and Giff lay still for almost ten minutes while he tried to press a bandage hard against the bleeding shoulder wound. He could not reach the exit hole where Jessie had extracted the bullet, but fortunately it was the entry hole which had torn open. When he finally did get the bleeding stopped, he felt a little weak. But the courtyard was just below, and when he raised his head he could see Castillo upstairs in his bedroom. The man was with a woman and their laughter was sharp and ribald.

Giff steeled himself and eased over the wall. He dropped into the courtyard and grunted softly as pain shot up his side. For a moment he knelt in the flowers feeling waves of dizziness pass over him. Then he came to his feet and leaned against the wall. *I have got to do better than this,* he thought angrily. *I have to ignore the pain and the weakness or I haven't a chance. With Pa dead, Maria's life now depends on me alone!*

Giff pictured how his half-sister might look. How any pretty girl looks at the age of sixteen. And then he thought of all the years she had been a slave to some rich man and how that man might already have violated her. Giff used the fabricated image of Maria's soiled innocence to goad himself into a fury that trespassed the boundaries of his own pain. He stood up straight and moved silently across the courtyard. He entered the huge *casa* and slipped behind some drapery as a fat maid padded heavily down the candlelit hallway. Giff could still hear Castillo's laughter, and it made the ex–Texas Ranger's lip curl with contempt. After this night, Castillo would never laugh again, never use his power and influence to steal cattle and slaves from the United States and then have his men bring them across the border, where they would be swallowed up in the bowels of Old Mexico.

Giff eased out from behind the drapes. He saw a staircase leading up to the second floor and he went straight for it. Once, as he climbed the stairs, he thought he sensed a movement behind him, and he whirled but saw nothing. He continued on with his sixgun gripped tightly in his fist.

Just before he reached the top of the stairs, the girl with Castillo cried out sharply in pain. No longer laughing, her voice took on a pleading quality that made Giff hurry down the hallway. When Giff came to a halt outside Castillo's door, the girl was almost crying.

"All right, you sonofabitch," Giff whispered, "it's payoff time!"

He shoved open the door. In the candlelit room, he had a split-second image of Castillo, naked, with a whip in his fist, standing over the equally naked Mexican girl, who had been roped to his four bedposts.

"Fun and games are over," Giff hissed, cocking his six-gun.

Castillo did something totally unexpected. He slashed downward with the whip and the girl screamed in pain.

Giff jumped forward as Castillo raised the whip again. The Mexican brought the whip up, and its leather bit into Giff's cheek, drawing blood. Before Giff could pistol-whip Castillo, the man had ducked under his arms and was racing for the doorway.

Giff swore and triggered off a shot. He shot only to wound Castillo, because the man might be the only living person who knew where Maria was being kept. His bullet clipped Castillo across his buttocks and the man howled as he disappeared into the hallway. To make things even worse, the poor damned girl just kept screaming over and over. "Shut up!" Giff roared, "I came to save your ass, not use it!"

The girl did not understand English. She was very young and frightened. Giff swore and jumped for the doorway. He had totally botched this job, and if he didn't act fast Castillo would be out of his reach in seconds.

Giff raced to the top of the stairway and started down the steps, taking them three at a time. But halfway down, he caught his boot-heel and tripped. He tried to catch his balance but when he crashed down and slammed his bad shoulder into the stone steps, his gun went flying and he blacked out still hearing the stupid señorita's screams ringing in his ears.

He awoke sometime in the night as a shiver of pain shot through his body. Dimly, he struggled to open his eyes. When he did, he saw a lean, hawk-faced Mexican draw back his fist. Giff tried to duck the blow, but that was when he realized that he was suspended by his wrists and hanging from the rafters about a foot off the floor. The fist exploded against his cheekbone and he lost consciousness again.

"Wake up!" the already familiar voice of Antonio Castillo demanded.

Giff felt a bucket of cold water splash into his face. He gagged and coughed but saw no reason to open his eyes.

"Again, Rodrigo!"

Giff felt his head rock back as the one called Rodrigo smashed him a second time. A moment later, another bucket of cold water was splashed into his face. Giff opened his eyes and tried to focus on the man who stood before him.

Antonio Castillo was fully dressed now. He looked pale and in pain, however; and Giff allowed himself the luxury of thinking he was the cause of Castillo's great discomfort.

"How's your wounded ass feeling, Antonio?" Giff taunted through battered lips. "Gonna be a while until you ride a horse or a woman again, huh?"

Castillo flung himself at Giff. The Texan brought his knee up and drove it into Castillo's groin. The man went hysterical. It would have been a damned good show if Rodrigo hadn't started using his fists again.

Chapter 16

It was well after midnight when Jessie arrived in Juarez and rode toward Don Castillo's front gate. She assumed that Giff would have scaled the wall, a feat which she did not believe she could accomplish. And she was equally certain that she would be remembered by the pair of guards who had been standing at the gates the last time she had entered.

So how was she to gain access to the guarded stronghold of Antonio Castillo? Jessie considered the problem very carefully. She certainly could not hope to storm the gates and get through, because, even if she did accomplish that much, Castillo would be alerted and his men would shoot or capture her at once.

Jessie decided her only hope was to stage a diversion. One that the guards would almost certainly be attracted to. She could think of only two things that were certain to divert the guards—women and tequila.

She had little trouble finding both commodities in Juarez. At a *cantina* there were several prostitutes hanging around in the street. It saddened Jessie to see them but what had to be done tonight would be necessary in order to save lives. If the guards could be fully distracted, they would not have to be shot. Better this way than to spill more blood.

Jessie rode up to the *cantina* but she did not dismount. Almost at once, the women stopped talking and, in her halting Spanish, Jessie pointed at the two best looking of the group and said, *"Dos prostituta, dos botella tequila."* Then, as the women began to study her intently, Jessie held up two ten-dollar gold pieces and motioned toward the hill where Don Castillo lived. She wished she knew the name for "guards" but she figured that she could get the message across once she got the two women up near the gates.

At the sight of what was to them certainly a great deal of money, the two women straightened a little, pushed out their chests and swayed forward. Now Jessie dismounted. She kept the gold pieces but had some pesos which she used to indicate that one of the girls was to go for the two bottles of tequila.

The dark, sensuous women were both attractive and intelligent. In less than fifteen minutes, they were on their way, Jessie walking on foot beside them as they swung in close to the gates yet stayed behind a crumbling rock wall where they could not be seen. Jessie tied Sun up and, once more, using her broken Spanish and pantomiming her needs, she went over what the two women were supposed to do to earn their gold. The women giggled and seemed very excited about this and acted as if it were some kind of game. Jessie assumed the women might be able to get the guards drunk and earn even more money.

Hoping that she was doing the right thing, unable to figure out any other way to save Giff if he had fallen into Castillo's hands, Jessie paid the two young women and sent them sashaying up to the gates. Any doubts that she was dealing with professionals were soon dispelled as the women began to pretend they were already a little drunk. They giggled loudly and swayed their hips as they approached the guards. Laughing and prancing, they offered the men drinks and the pair of guards took the bottles and tipped them toward the moon. They laughed as if they had struck gold and then they each chose one of the women and began to hug and fondle them.

Jessie turned her back and hoped the women remembered that they had to lure the guards away from the gate so that she could enter and depart with Giff. The women remembered quite well. Taking the guards by the arms, they led them down the hill into the shadows. Jessie hurried through the gate. From what little Spanish she knew, it sounded as if the two couples were already getting right down to the basics. Jessie had tried to explain that the two women needed to keep the guards fully occupied for at least an hour. But given the way things were going, she supposed she might have a lot less time than that.

She was very careful as she entered the house. Almost at once she heard the unmistakable sound of flesh striking flesh. Jessie drew her gun and hurried forward. A heavy-set maid blundered out into her path and Jessie put her lips to her mouth. The maid covered her mouth, lifted her skirts and ran for her life.

Jessie hurried on. When she came to the room where the noises had originated she wasted no time but stepped into the open doorway and saw Castillo and his man Rodrigo standing before the unconscious form of Giff Jones, who hung like a carcass from the ceiling.

"One move and you're both dead," she told them in a voice that shook with barely controlled fury.

Rodrigo Lopez spun around but he saw the look in Jessie's eyes and his gun hand froze an inch over the handle of his weapon.

Castillo moved more slowly. He turned and regarded Jessie with unconcealed hatred. "So," he said, mocking her with his words and his perfect English diction, "you have missed me and decided that you want another try at my bed."

Jessie laughed out loud at his arrogance, but she did admire his control. "Cut my friend down," she whispered. "Cut him down and rouse him."

"Rodrigo, do as the lady says."

Rodrigo clearly did not want to follow these orders. "If we do that, then—"

Jessie interrupted. "No," she said, "if you *don't* do that, then you will both die."

"Ah," Castillo said, "but so will you. How did you get past my guards? Did you also promise them your favors?"

"Cut him down," Jessie repeated.

Rodrigo had little choice but to comply with her wishes.

"Now give him some of that rum you have on the counter," Jessie ordered. "Hurry!"

"Do as she says, Rodrigo. The woman is accustomed to giving orders."

Jessie did not like the taunting tone in Castillo's voice but she wasn't about to let the man rattle or distract her. She watched as Rodrigo cut Giff down. It made her so furious to see what they had done to Giff's face that she wanted to kill them both. "Now the rum," she said.

Giff came awake almost at once. He choked and his eyes fluttered open. It seemed to take him several minutes before he realized that he was no longer hanging from the ceiling and that Jessie had come to save his hide. When he did recover his senses, he stood up, a good head taller than either Rodrigo or Castillo. Without warning, he doubled up his fist and smashed Rodrigo square in the face. Jessie heard the Mexican's nose crunch. Then the man was skidding across the floor to lie unconscious.

"Now it's your turn," Giff said, turning on Castillo.

The man's composure bled away and he tried to retreat, only he came up against a wall and could go no farther.

"Giff," Jessie warned when the big man hammered Castillo to his knees. "Don't kill him! He's the only one who might know where your sister is."

It took a visible effort for Giff to pull himself under control and not grab Castillo by his neck and wring it like that of a chicken. "Get up!" Giff rasped.

Castillo was down. He crawled to his feet but did not want to climb erect until Giff grabbed a fistful of his hair and hauled him upright. "Where is my sister?" he demanded in a terrible voice.

Castillo was almost in a panic, yet, he whispered, "Please, señor, I do not know where she is!"

Giff wasn't buying it. He drove an uppercut from knee level that lifted Antonio Castillo a good foot off the ground. The man went pale and fell to all fours. "No more," he cried weakly. "Please, no more!"

"You've got five seconds to tell us where we can find my sister."

"She's dead," Castillo wheezed. "She's dead."

Giff hit the man so hard he bounced off the floor. "Don't do that!" Jessie cried. "He's no help to you if he's dead, and now he's unconscious."

Giff seemed to shake himself like a wet dog. "I want to kill him," he breathed, "I want to kill him more than I've ever wanted anything in this world."

Jessie stepped between the two men. "Let's take him hostage while we go to find your sister," she said. "If we do that, he'll have no choice but to break down and tell us what we need to know. It's the only hope you'll ever have of finding Maria."

Giff nodded. "All right," he said, glancing over at Rodrigo Lopez, knowing that he really ought to kill him or he'd be on their backtrail.

Jessie read his dark thoughts. "We do what we can to save your sister, but that doesn't include murder. Let him be."

"He'll bring men after us. Probably go straight to the authorities as well as Castillo's outlaws. They'll be on our trail before this time tomorrow."

"I know," Jessie said. "But we'll lose them. They're not Apache trackers and how can they follow us when even *we* don't know where we're going?"

"I hadn't thought of it that way," Giff admitted, reaching down and grabbing Antonio by the pants-leg. "All right, let's see if we can haul this carrion out of here."

He dragged Castillo out of the room and down the hallway. *Thank God,* Jessie thought, *we are not on the upper floor. If we were, he'd beat Castillo's brains out dragging him downstairs.*

There were fine horses in Castillo's stable and there was no one awake at this hour of the night to stop them from being taken. As Jessie and Giff rode out with Don Castillo hanging over the back of a blooded animal, they were unopposed and unnoticed.

"Where are the guards?" Giff asked.

"They're well taken care of," Jessie said. "Don't worry about them."

Right then, they both heard a woman giggling drunkenly and a man snoring very loud. Jessie rode off a ways into the darkness and when she came upon a prostrate couple, she took a moment to warn the prostitute to get her friend and leave before daylight or they could be in trouble.

The woman thanked her and rose unsteadily to her feet. Jessie watched her march over to the dim outline of another sleeping couple. She roused her friend and they linked arms. Weaving and singing happily, the two women slowly trudged down the hill back to Juarez. No doubt it was a night that they would long remember.

"Where are we going now?" Jessie asked as she rejoined Giff and then rode over to remount Sun.

"Good question." Giff squinted up at the stars. His rugged face was badly swollen and cut. It would be a while before he looked normal, and in the moonlight he appeared almost frightening. "My guess would be to take to the river and follow it downstream until daybreak, just to throw anyone off our tracks."

"And then?"

"Then we hole up until Castillo either tells me where to find my sister or I kill him."

Jessie shuddered, for she knew that she could not stop Giff from carrying out his threat. "He said she was dead."

"He's a damned liar!" Giff choked. "Why should anyone believe a man like him?"

"No reason."

Giff took a deep breath and got a hold on his emotions. "I didn't mean to yell at you," he said in apology. "Let's ride for the river. We'll face what to do when tomorrow comes."

Jessie agreed that sounded like a good idea. She was too weary to think about much. A night of lovemaking followed by a night of walking to El Paso and then rescuing Giff had left her feeling mighty tired. And tomorrow she would feel even worse. But maybe Maria Jones was close and they could get Castillo to tell them where she was before Giff actually did lose his temper and throttle the man.

Castillo was not the bravest person in the world. Jessie figured that if he wasn't really telling them the awful truth about Maria, the rich Mexican would crack.

Chapter 17

Dawn found them fifteen miles below Juarez, holed up in a grove of cottonwood trees. Jessie had only closed her eyes a moment, and yet when she opened them again she was surprised to see that the sun was high. She knew she would have slept all day had it not been for the fact that Giff was sitting on Castillo's sunken chest with a red-hot poker in his hand. And if Castillo had not been gagged, he would have been heard in Austin.

Jessie wanted to shout at Giff, but something told her that the man would only push Castillo all the harder if he thought she was trying to interfere.

Giff, face banged up and eyes as hard as granite rock, said, "All right, Castillo, we've come to the moment of truth. You're either going to tell us where my sister is living, or I'm going to slap a big old brand right square in the middle of your forehead. And if that doesn't fry your brain, then I'll brand each one of your cheeks. And if you still won't tell me the truth then I'll take and cut your ears off and toss 'em in the river for the catfish to eat. They like human ears about as well as anything you could imagine."

Giff shoved the smoldering poker at Castillo, who looked like an overstuffed worm trying to twist its way into the earth. Jessie watched with rising anxiety.

Giff withdrew the poker from between Castillo's eyes. "Are you ready to sing out the truth now?"

Castillo nodded madly.

Giff pulled the gag from his mouth, only instead of singing Castillo bellowed for help. Giff shoved the bandage back into his mouth and lightly touched the poker to Castillo's forehead. The man screeched and then fainted.

"Giff!"

"I barely touched him," Giff said, "only he don't know that. To him, it feels as if I burned a deep hole in his forehead. When he wakes up, he'll think his brains must be running out."

Jessie shuddered. She could see now that there was a large blister rising on Castillo's forehead but that Castillo's flesh wasn't charred or even burned too badly. "I'll get some water."

She came back with a canteen full of river water and Giff poured it directly onto Castillo's face. "Wake up, señor," Giff growled. "The party is just getting started."

Castillo obviously did not want to regain consciousness just yet. He struggled feebly under Giff's weight, but when water ran down his nostrils, he began to cough.

Giff reached for the poker again. It had lost its cherry color but it was still hot enough to burn flesh. "Now," Giff said, "before I do your right cheek, where is my sister?"

Castillo was broken. "In the village of Coban!"

Giff pulled the poker back. "Where the hell is Coban?"

"In the mountains, deep in Mexico," Castillo wheezed.

Giff shoved the poker back in his face. "Exactly where are these damned mountains you speak of?"

"They are far to the south. You have heard of the city of Torreón?"

"Yes," Giff said.

"That is where she is being held. I swear this is true, señor!"

"He's telling you the truth," Jessie said. "I've heard of those mountains myself."

172

"If you're lying," Giff whispered, climbing off Castillo and tossing the poker back into his campfire, "I will make you suffer a thousand deaths."

"I do not lie! She is being held by a rich man. A terrible man. I was trying to get her away for your father. But . . ." Antonio Castillo held his hands up in a gesture of futility.

"How many days' travel?" Giff asked.

"A week. No more."

"What about your man? Does he know this is the place my sister is being held?"

"No, señor! He knows nothing. It would not have served my purposes to give Rodrigo Lopez such valuable knowledge."

Jessie did not believe him for a minute and neither did Giff, but there was no sense in making an issue of it. If Rodrigo Lopez and the Mexican authorities were going to ride all the way down to Coban, nothing was going to stop them. Jessie figured that she and Giff would just have to assume that men were on their backtrail and be ready to act accordingly.

"Castillo," Giff said in a voice so soft it was chilling, "If your man comes with either *banditos* or the authorities, you will be the first one to die. They might get us, but I swear you will die in agony. Is that understood?"

Castillo covered his face with his hands and wept. "I do not want to die," he managed to say. "I have much to pay you. I can help you get your sister back safely."

"Do that," Jessie said, "and you have my word that we will repay you with your life." She looked right at Giff. "Is this agreeable with you?"

Giff nodded. He poured Jessie a cup of coffee, ignoring Castillo, who seemed very content to be ignored. "Then we leave at once for Coban."

"What about Ki?" she asked.

Giff found a cigarillo in his shirt pocket. He lit it, using a smoldering brand from the campfire, and inhaled deeply before he spoke. "Jessie, I've waited a lot of years for the chance to see my sister again. I don't even remember her face, but I know she was beautiful. I'm going on but I sure wouldn't hold it against you to turn back and wait for Ki in El Paso. In fact, I'd rest easier in my mind if you *did* return to Texas."

"We could both wait for Ki," she said.

"Uh-uh." Giff's bruised face softened. "You know that Castillo's lieutenant is already on our trail. Because of this river, he'll lose it. So then what can he do but make the perfectly reasonable assumption that I'll be heading for Coban? The way I see it, about the only chance I have of getting Maria out of Mexico is to get to her before anyone else does. That's why we took Castillo's best horses, horses swift enough to match that palomino you ride. It's got to be a race, Jessie. You know I can't wait for your samurai to show up."

Jessie realized that this was true, though the idea of going hundreds of miles into Mexico with either outlaws or bandits on their trail was not appealing. And yet the idea of leaving Giff to go alone was even worse. Besides, there was a young girl whose future was at stake. A girl who had long ago been kidnapped by raiders and sold into slavery. A girl named Maria who had a right to live free and with a chance at happiness.

"I'm coming," Jessie said. "I'll start saddling my horse right now."

Giff reached out and pulled her close, looking very concerned. "Are you sure, Jessie? I don't want to have to worry about ... I mean, if anything happened to you, I'd ..."

She kissed his swollen lips very tenderly. "I'm sure."

He looked into her eyes and then he said no more.

Jessie had thought southwestern Texas was hard country, but she now learned that northern Mexico was even worse. They rode through some of the most useless, bitter land that she had ever seen in her life. Land that reminded her of the Sonora Desert in Arizona. Land that offered nothing to a human being except a lingering death. And yet sometimes a river would suddenly appear as if by magic. It might run for fifty miles or more and leave a valley of life where simple peasants worked their crops and raised their families. These small villages were the heart of Mexico, the true country. Jessie saw families that lived in small, one-room adobe huts that looked as if they were ready to fall in and leave the family with absolutely nothing. But the people she saw looked happy. The old ones sat in front of the hovels and ground corn or weaved wool and cotton into clothing. The middle-aged ones raised children or worked in their fields. The children played stick-ball games with balls made of leather filled with wool. The dogs were thin, and yet, like the people, they smiled at the strangers and gazed at them with curiosity.

"How can a man like you be so rich and not feel something for your fellow countrymen who are so poor?" Jessie asked Antonio Castillo.

"They know no better than this, so they are happy," was the reply.

"Then you feel no guilt?" Jessie asked.

"They are of Indian blood. I am of Spanish blood. I have no obligation to them. They are born, they grow old, and then they die, leaving nothing, giving nothing."

Even Giff, who had seen more than his share of hard

living, was annoyed by such a callous remark. "They are people like yourself, Castillo. Not cattle. They love their children and their families."

"I wish them no harm," Castillo muttered.

"Is that true?" Giff countered. "Your outlaws prey on these villages just like a pack of wolves against a flock of helpless sheep. They rape the women and steal the corn and livestock. They take slaves and then they sell them in faraway places like Mexico City and Guatemala."

"They are Indians," Castillo repeated, his voice hard and uncompromising. "If the life out here is too hard, then they should go to the cities and seek work. Only animals would live like this."

Jessie could not stomach such a man and she mounted Sun in anger, then rode on feeling as if she could never understand someone like Castillo.

Several hard days later, they approached a lovely valley where the river flowed through grassy meadows. They saw a large mission and heard bells in the distance. When Jessie squinted her eyes, she saw that the bells were being rung by a group of sisters in what appeared to be a convent.

"Where are we?" Jessie asked.

Both men shrugged their shoulders. "These little villages don't even have names. There can't be more than five hundred people here," Giff said.

Jessie said nothing more as they rode into the settlement. It looked quite old. There was a plaza with big shade trees and a water well in the middle. Upon their arrival, the citizens stopped and gawked at them curiously. A priest left the mission and hurried away with a young boy tugging on his sleeve. He was dressed in shabby purple vestments and he wore a silver and turquoise crucifix around his neck.

Observing it, Giff said, "I'm surprised that your outlaws have not taken that crucifix and sold it to the devil."

Castillo's dark blue eyes grew flinty. "I am not the one who does those things, but only a fool wears his wealth. A wiser priest would put that away where it could not be found."

They stopped at a watering place and let the horses drink. The day was very hot and the night was quickly approaching. "How many more miles can we go today?" Jessie asked.

Giff must have read the weariness in her voice. "I think we can afford to spend the night in this village," he said, studying it closely and deciding that there was no danger.

Jessie dismounted, heavy with trail-weariness. They had been riding steadily for six days. Sun was holding up well, but she could count his ribs and almost feel his backbone through her saddle. "Castillo, call for someone to come and care for the horses."

"Anyone in particular?" he asked sarcastically.

Giff reached out and grabbed him by the collar, then shook him like a terrier would a rat. "Just call it out and offer ten pesos."

Castillo did as they ordered, though it was clear he thought this task was far beneath his dignity; he wanted nothing to do with these peons.

Almost immediately, nearly a dozen men appeared, each with his simple straw hat clenched in his hand, and each very eager to earn such a great sum of money.

"Now what are we going to do?" Giff asked.

Jessie frowned. "Give them all a peso and tell them they must each help get feed and water, then take turns standing guard over the animals right here in this plaza until we ride out tomorrow morning."

"Good idea," Giff said. "Tell them, Castillo. And keep

in mind that both Jessie and I know enough Spanish to keep things honest. If you try to tell them anything different, you're in deep trouble."

Castillo understood. He told the peons exactly what Jessie had instructed and they went into sort of a noisy huddle. Jessie watched with unconcealed amusement as they suddenly all raced off to find grass and grain. In a very few minutes, they had returned and were unsaddling the horses and hauling buckets of water for them.

"In these parts," Giff said, "a man still gets a little service for his money."

When the horses were taken care of and a rope corral had been rigged up around them in the center of the plaza, Jessie paid the men, who humbly bowed to with gratitude.

"I just hope they don't give it all to the priest," Giff grumbled. Jessie had noticed that Giff did not think much of priests and nuns, or for that matter, any clergy. He seemed to consider them partly responsible for the poverty of people. He thought religion was an opiate. This disturbed Jessie, but it was not an uncommon attitude among men who were accustomed to wresting whatever they got out of life by force.

Jessie turned back to Castillo. "Now," she said, "call the women and offer another peso to each if they will bring food and drink."

"I do not deal with women like these!"

Giff backhanded Castillo and he went sprawling into the dirt. "Maybe if you had known a few decent women, you'd have turned out worth something, dammit! Now do as Jessie says and don't give us any of your back-talk!"

Castillo climbed to his feet. He brushed the dust off his clothes and wiped a smear of blood from the corner of his lips. Aware that the entire village was watching, he tried to put on a bluster, but under Giff's hard stare it fizzled out completely. So he called the women, who were delighted to also earn a peso. And in no time at all, they had tortillas, corn, and beans, more than they could possibly eat.

"Delicious," Jessie said.

"Twenty pesos has got to be the biggest damned payday this village has ever seen. These people will pray that we come riding through on our way back to Texas."

"Then we shall answer their prayers," Jessie said. "Please ask them the name of this lovely village."

Castillo asked.

A man who looked to be one of the leaders of the village smiled broadly. "Coban," he said. "Coban."

"Jesus Christ!" Giff whispered. "This is the place!" He grabbed Castillo by the collar and drew him up on his toes. "Where were you taking us?"

"I didn't know! I swear I didn't! Why should a man like me come to a place such as this!"

Castillo's question reflected such an innate degree of arrogance that both Jessie and Giff knew that it was the truth.

Giff shoved the rich Mexican aside and turned to the peon, who looked frightened by what he had just seen. "Where's Maria Jones?" Giff whispered. *"Donde está Maria Jones!"*

When the peon began to retreat in fear, Giff grabbed him by the shoulders and Jessie jumped between them. "Giff, you're frightening the poor man!"

Giff released him and took a deep breath. *"Por favor,"* he whispered, *"donde está Maria?"*

The Mexican looked at Jessie, who smiled with encouragement and nodded. Reassured, the villager pointed up at the hill where they had seen the convent.

"No!" Giff shouted as comprehension dawned on him. "He doesn't understand!" Giff shoved Castillo forward.

"Make him understand, damn you!" he yelled, shoving his gun into Castillo's back.

Castillo spoke so rapidly they could not understand him. But the peon obviously understood perfectly and, again, he pointed up at the convent.

Giff seemed to shiver. "Dammit, Maria!" he whispered, as he strode to his horse. "Goddammit, no!"

He grabbed the reins of one of the saddled horses and swung up onto its back and raced toward the convent.

"Giff!" Jessie shouted, turning to grab Sun only to see Castillo escaping across the plaza as the Mexicans stared in bewilderment.

Jessie could have shot Castillo before he vanished, but she realized that was the only way she was going to stop the man. Unwilling to kill him, she had little choice but to grab her own saddle and throw it on Sun's back. She mounted quickly and touched spurs to the palomino's sweat-caked sides.

No one had to tell her that she better be present if Giff discovered his only living relative had become a nun. Yes, she had better be there or Giff might say something that would forever scar his soul.

Chapter 18

Jessie raced up the hill, spurring Sun to his maximum speed. They passed the priest, who was hurrying on foot in the same direction. Jessie had a bad feeling. The priest was clearly disturbed, and he was too fat to be hurrying in this heat up the hillside unless called by some emergency. Jessie prayed that no ill had fallen upon Maria Jones. What a terrible stroke of fate it would be to have her die just minutes before her brother could reach her side. Maybe the same thought had occurred to Giff, because he almost killed his horse in a mad rush to reach the convent grounds. Even so, Jessie's palomino slowly gained ground on Giff Jones, so that when he flew into the yard scattering both chickens and nuns she was right at his side.

Giff vaulted out of the saddle and yelled, "Maria! Maria Jones!"

Jessie raced to his side. She could see the nuns were upset. Several were crying and it was all that Jessie could do to hold Giff until he regained his senses. "For God's sake, use your head! The priest will be along in a moment. You can't go—"

But Giff wasn't listening. He pulled away from Jessie and strode toward a small, vine-covered chapel where he could hear singing. Bursting into the chapel, he saw a casket lying open before the altar. He froze for just a moment, and Jessie caught up with him. She took his arm and she could actually feel him trembling with dread. She waited a moment, and when he stumbled forward, she went at his side.

It was only perhaps fifteen feet to the altar, past the worn benches and the stations of the cross, past the other nuns, who wore beautiful black lace mantillas and who prayed fervently for the soul of the deceased. Giff stopped before the casket and steeled himself, then looked down.

The casket contained a very old and beautiful Mexican woman. Jessie heard Giff expel a sigh of relief. He staggered and took a seat on the bench and bowed his head for a moment, though Jessie doubted if it were in prayer. Suddenly, a soft voice and slender hand touched his shoulder. "I am Sister Maria," the young woman said.

Giff turned his face upward and looked into her blue eyes. "I am your brother, Giff," he whispered. "I came to take you home."

She smiled. "First we must pray for Mother Nuella, who served us for twenty years and was like my own mother. I loved her deeply."

Before Giff could rise or even form a protest on his lips, Sister Maria walked to the altar and knelt. Jessie could hear the whisper of her prayers; then the priest arrived to kneel by her side. The nuns filed into the chapel, filling its seats, and then the priest arose and they began to recite the rosary.

Giff waited for his sister almost an hour. When she finally arose from the hard stone floor, he followed her outside while Jessie listened to the long funeral mass. When it was over, she walked outside to see Giff and his sister standing beside the horses.

Jessie walked over to join them. Giff looked devastated. "She says she has been asked by the priest to assume the Mother's position of responsibility here. She says she cannot come back to Texas with us, Jessie. Never."

This decision was not unexpected. She only had to look into Sister Maria's serene eyes to know that the young woman had found beauty and peace attending to her God and the people of Coban. Sister Maria was tall, like her brother, but her features were different, reflecting her Mexican heritage. She spoke no English and was quite pretty. There was an aura of well-being and happiness about her that Jessie had seen only in a very few people.

Jessie took Giff's arm. "Did you tell her about her father?"

"Yes. She said she would pray for him, too."

"I see. Why don't you tell her that you will come back some day to visit."

Giff studied Jessie for a long moment. "Yes," he said finally. "I can see that this is a bad time. I should come back in a few years. Maybe then I can help her in some way."

"I'm sure you can."

Jessie mounted Sun and rode off a ways to wait. She did not wait long. Giff soon came riding up to her. When he turned back toward the convent, he waved to his sister for the last time. "She was also beautiful," he said reverently. "And very happy, I think."

"I *know* she was happy, Giff."

They rode slowly down the hill to the plaza. Giff did not ask about Antonio Castillo, and Jessie did not mention the man's name. After all, he had brought them to this town and the young nun, and they had promised to spare his life for that task.

Giff unsaddled his horse. "If it is all right with you, Jessie, I'd like to turn back early in the morning."

"I'd like that fine. Shall we sleep out here with our horses in this plaza or . . ."

"No," he said quickly. "I want to hold you tonight. Make love to you, Jessie."

She nodded and was glad.

"Jessie, wake up!"

Jessie started out of a deep sleep. So did Giff, who lay at her side. She blinked into the candlelight. "Ki? Ki!"

The samurai was standing over them. "There are outlaws coming this way," he said. "Castillo rode north and intercepted them."

Giff sprang to his feet and buckled on his gunbelt. "This is Maria's village," he grated.

Jessie also dressed quickly. "How many, Ki?"

"Far too many," the samurai told her.

Giff shook his head stubbornly. "I'll fight them to the death!" He strode out of the room and across the plaza, his spurs noisily raking the hard-packed dirt. Jessie looked at Ki and they both went for their horses, but Giff was already saddled and riding north to meet Castillo and his outlaws before they were ready to join him.

"How far away?" Jessie asked as she worked frantically to cinch her horse tight.

"About five miles. I didn't know where you and Giff went after leaving Casa Castillo. So I followed Rodrigo Lopez and they brought me to this village."

Jessie mounted her horse. The peon who had been holding her bit stepped back and made the sign of the cross, then whispered, "*Adios, señorita!*"

"*Adios,*" she told him as she galloped north with Ki at her side.

Before they had ridden two miles they heard a quick succession of rifle shots and then a scattered volley. Jessie raced Sun forward, and when she flew over a low hill, she saw Giff. He was down behind a fallen tree and under a heavy fire from his enemies. Had it been broad daylight, he wouldn't have lasted a minute.

Jessie and Ki dismounted and, dodging their way through a hail of bullets, joined him.

Giff turned to them. "There was just enough moonlight to see that peacock Castillo. I got him through the heart with my first bullet. Rodrigo Lopez was at his side and he took my second. That's them lying there in the field, along with a couple more for good measure."

Jessie looked to see the silhouettes of the still bodies. "But how many more are there?" Jessie asked. She had counted at least thirty separate muzzle flashes since she had joined Giff.

"I don't know, nor did I give a goddamn!" Giff shouted, firing rapidly, though for every shot he triggered, ten were fired back in deadly reply.

In the moonlight, Jessie looked at Ki. He read her dark thoughts. To remain here and fight was to die just as surely as the sun was going to rise again tomorrow.

"Giff, let's get out of here to fight again," Jessie pleaded. "We can't change things down here. They won't hurt a nun, and they'd be cutting their own livelihood off if they burned the village."

"I want to finish off every damn one of them!" Giff cried hoarsely.

Jessie took a deep breath and nodded to the samurai. Ki understood. He reached over and his powerful thumb dug into Giff's thick neck. Giff tried to swing his rifle around, but Jessie whacked him across the skull with her pistol, and he folded.

"Let's throw him back across the horse and put some miles between us and them before sunrise," she said.

And that's what they did. Dawn found them thirty miles north of Coban, running for the Texas border. Their horses were too fast to be overtaken and, in Jessie's opinion, Giff was going to be their greatest threat when he regained consciousness. This was the third time that they had tied the big man across his saddle. He would be filled with outrage, and maybe would even want to fight the samurai once again.

But Ki could take care of himself, and until Giff realized that Texas and the Rangers needed a man of his caliber, Jessie would take care of him. And if he was real lucky, some day he could return to the heart of Mexico and get to know his sister. Maybe, if that happened, some of the wildness would leave him and he would find some peace in this world before his days ran out.

Jessie hoped so. Giff Jones was a man worth saving.